THE SURLY SULLEN BELL

by RUSSELL KIRK

Russell Kirk, who gained the acclaim of the nation recently with his Gothick novel, OLD HOUSE OF FEAR, now tops the thrills of that widely praised *tour de force* with his intensely realistic ghost stories. Writing from his haunted house at Mecosta, Michigan, one of the most isolated places on earth, Dr. Kirk takes you on eerie trips to visit deconsecrated churches, the drawing room of a poisoner, ancient cellars, Scottish castles, deserted houses off lonely roads, and the most fascinating of all—the great, almost uninhabited wilderness. There is the chilling speculation of a major thinker behind each of these tales, and the vengeful ghosts of Russell Kirk select their contemporary victims with proper morbid care.

In his Foreword, Dr. Kirk says, "More of the outer darkness than of the twilight zone, these tales are unabashedly Gothick. In them the reader may find hints of M. R. James, Henry James, and even Jesse James. I have no theory to account for ghosts: I merely recognize the existence of such phenomena . . . if I am asked whether I have ever perceived a ghost—why, I would be a poor dull creature if I hadn't, considering the places where I have gone and stock I come from."

No.

THE SURLY SULLEN BELL

Fiction by Russell Kirk

THE SURLY SULLEN BELL

OLD HOUSE OF FEAR

THE SURLY SULLEN BELL

TEN STORIES AND SKETCHES, UNCANNY OR UNCOMFORTABLE, WITH A NOTE ON THE GHOSTLY TALE BY

🔔 *Russell Kirk*

FLEET PUBLISHING CORPORATION
230 PARK AVENUE, NEW YORK, N.Y.

To Miss Gracia Virgo, Witch of Saginaw,
from the Wizard of Mecosta

Foreword

More of the outer darkness than of the twilight zone, these are tales unabashedly Gothick. In them the reader may find hints of M. R. James, Henry James, and even Jesse James. I have no theory to account for ghosts and kindred bogles: I merely recognize the existence of such phenomena, as do a good many psychologists nowadays.

Much of my life has been spent in haunted places: in the most ghostly of towns, St. Andrews; in the Isle of Eigg, or the back lanes of Verona and Rome; in the curious castles and country houses of Fife; and especially in my own creaking old house at Mecosta, in Michigan, pervaded by the Swedenborgian genius of my ancestors.

Turning up frequently in these pages, the *revenant* may come to seem almost natural, not to say cozy. Yet he is, after all, the most common and satisfactory sort of spectre. In all these stories, there resides some grain or kernel of fact; but only the concluding sketch, "Lost Lake," is a True Narration.

If I am asked whether I have ever perceived a ghost—why, I would be a poor dull creature if I hadn't, considering the places where I have gone and the stock from which I come. But the True Narration of this sort rarely succeeds as a work of literary art: it is too fragmentary and inconclusive. Some day I may collect my rags and tags of True Narration, whether my own experiences or reliable accounts from people I know well. But that will be another book than this.

Aside from "The Cellar of Little Egypt" (of which, by the way, most of the characters did live and some of the episodes did occur) these tales have been published over the past decades in English, Canadian, and American periodicals: *World Review, Queen's Quarterly, The London Mystery Magazine, Fantasy and Science Fiction,* and *Southwest Review.*

There is appended a note on the ghostly tale in English letters, previously printed in *The Critic.*

RUSSELL KIRK
Piety Hill
Mecosta, Michigan

CONTENTS

♭

Foreword — vii

UNCLE ISAIAH — 11

OFF THE SAND ROAD — 37

EX TENEBRIS — 55

THE SURLY SULLEN BELL — 77

THE CELLAR OF LITTLE EGYPT — 105

SKYBERIA — 129

SORWORTH PLACE — 143

BEHIND THE STUMPS — 169

WHAT SHADOWS WE PURSUE — 191

LOST LAKE — 217

A Cautionary Note on the Ghostly Tale — 231

UNCLE ISAIAH

🔔

"And behold, at eveningtide trouble; and before the morning he is not. This is the portion of them that spoil us, and the lot of them that rob us."
—Isa. 17:14.

One dusty evening, as the newsboys began to shout "Racing Final!" just before the shop's closing time, a squat man pushed into Kinnaird's Cleaners and demanded twenty dollars a week. Daniel Kinnaird blinked his mild eyes and looked at the card the squat man gave him, and shook his head. "You'll come across," said the squat man, in a gin voice. "Costa's out. They all come through." He grinned savagely. "I'll be back tomorrow, collecting." Before Daniel Kinnaird could think of anything to reply, the squat man had waddled back into the crowd in the street and had been swept away.

"North End Cleaners Prudential Association," the card read. It was a neat white card, but Daniel Kinnaird caught a whiff of the stench-bombs for which it was ambassador: the splintering plate-glass, the explosion, the greasy smoke, the intolerable stench.

Kinnaird's Cleaners, Dyers and Tailors, Unusual Service, occupied a square stone building with a quoined doorway that once had been handsome. Like most other business fronts in this street of the North End, it had been a gentleman's house, and Daniel Kinnaird could remember when half a dozen of these graceful mansions had remained as homes of old families. Now only one such was a home, and that, the building next door: the Kinnaird house. Everywhere else, slum children pounded up and down the stairs, or the old parlors were decorated with chromium and converted into hamburger-joints, or the ground-floor façades were knocked away to make room for car-wash garages. Fashionable suburbs, the automobile, and industrialization had turned the North End into a boneyard of defaced and degraded old houses.

But the Kinnairds remained. They had been among the first to come; they would be the last to go. Indeed, the Kinnairds *could* not go any longer, because their money had trickled away: the North End manacled them. Twenty years before, what remained of the Kinnaird capital had been invested in the dry-cleaning business, and at first this had been an enterprise modestly prospering. Today it was strangling. The pickup trucks of flashy, shoddy, cut-rate cleaners carried away half their custom; what trade survived came from the Italians and Poles and Negroes and nondescripts who packed the houses along this bleary ancient street—people who did their own pressing, brought cleaning only when they must, and required a tailor merely for patches.

Uncle Isaiah 13

After supper, Daniel Kinnaird blinked nightly over his ledgers. Kinnaird's Cleaners no longer could afford a bookkeeper; the help consisted of a girl at the counter, two pressers, a cleaner, and the old Russian Jew who had been their tailor ever since the business had been establishd. Kinnaird and his wife did all they could, yet every month receipts crept down just a trifle further. Though poor, Daniel Kinnaird was not cheap: his establishment cleaned clothes carefully, and when—at long intervals—some customer wanted a suit, that suit was tailored decently. So Kinnaird's Cleaners had become a depressed undertaking in a market where cheapness was the sole factor in competition. Kinnaird could not afford paying twenty dollars a week to the North End Cleaners Prudential Association. In any event it would have been wrong to pay. Old-fangled folk, the Kinnairds still judged in terms of right and wrong.

"Costa's out." Though Kinnaird did not read the newspapers thoroughly, he understood that. "Costa's out"—this was *finis* for Kinnaird's Cleaners, he supposed. Last week the governor had pardoned Bruno Costa, who had been serving concurrent sentences for extortion and assault with intent to do great bodily harm; but the governor had pardoned him after less than two years in the penitentiary. An election had been won, a new chief magistrate and new judges had been sworn into office, certain pre-election pledges had to be fulfilled. To the representatives of the Press, the governor had spoken in humanitarian fashion about modern concepts of penology, and had liberated six eminent thugs. Of these fortunate six, Costa was the least; but he was big enough to run the North End.

Kinnaird went into the tailor's room. Cross-legged on his

broad bench sat the old Jew, and Kinnaird handed him the card. "Oi, Mr. Kinnaird," said the tailor, raising his eyebrows in sympathy, "how much?"

"They want twenty dollars a week, Sol."

"Could be worse," the Jew told him, spreading his palms in resignation. "Could be worse, Mr. Kinnaird. You pay, yes? Always better to pay."

"No," said Daniel Kinnaird. "They never dared come near me before. What shall I do, Sol? Why do they come now?"

In a gesture of futility, the tailor protruded his lower lip. "Costa already got everybody else, Mr. Kinnaird. Kowalski's Drugs, on the corner, he pays. Jim's Garage, he pays. Every kind business, Costa got some association. I'm telling you, Mr. Kinnaird, better to pay. Costa's boys, they throw bombs, stink up the place; maybe they beat you, maybe me. To pay is better."

"I'll call the police," Daniel Kinnaird murmured, his inflection rising.

The Jew cackled joylessly. "Maybe Costa fix the police, maybe not. Maybe not; but anyhow, the police ain't got time for watching your front window day and night, Mr. Kinnaird."

"The Kinnairds don't pay people like Costa," Daniel Kinnaird said, mostly to himself.

"I'm telling you, it's bad times all over." The tailor shrugged; and then, rising suddenly, put on his coat. "At supper, you think it over. To pay is cheaper. Good night." He went softly out the back door; and Kinnaird, watching him through the window, observed that Sol glanced around the corner before he stepped into the darkening alley.

Closing time past, the rest of the help had gone home; so Kinnaird locked the doors with deliberation, took all the money from the till and tucked it inside his coat, and left the shop by the door in the wall which led into his house. This he locked and bolted, once he was in his hall, and put a chair against the knob. Picking up the telephone, he dialed the number of Hanchett, the bookseller, a laconic old man of some astuteness.

"Charles?" Kinnaird said. "A man came today from Costa. They want twenty dollars every week. What can I do?"

"Pay," came Hanchett's rasping voice.

"It wouldn't be right to pay. What else, Charles?"

"Do you know anybody in the rackets, anybody big?"

"No."

"No, you wouldn't." Hanchett coughed. "Well, if you did, you might persuade somebody to make Costa call it off. Do you know anybody in the City Hall?"

"No, and I don't want to."

"There fades your second chance, Daniel. I'll make it short and sour: you've got to know somebody *tough*. If you don't, you'll have to pay. If you need cash, I'll lend you some tomorrow." Hanchett hung up.

Daniel Kinnaird lingered by the telephone stand, staring at the cover of the directory. "For an emergency call to the police, dial 0," said a big black line of print. He shook his head and went into the kitchen, where his wife was at the stove. "Alma," he sighed, "please sit down a moment."

Having glanced at his face, tall Alma obeyed. "What is it?" He told her.

"Do we know anyone *tough*, Alma?" he asked, after

they had sat some time in silence, his wife with her hands against her temples.

"We might see Simonds, the alderman," she ventured.

"He knows we voted the wrong way," was all Kinnaird answered. She nodded, and for some minutes they listened to the clock's ticking.

"We'll have to manage to pay, that's all," Mrs. Kinnaird remarked then, as if she were angry with her husband.

"It's wrong to pay a man like Costa." He stared her down. "There's someone we might turn to, you know, Alma—"

Her thin lips parted, as if to ask "Who?" But she shut them tight before the word came out; and watching her husband's expression, she shook her gray head vigorously.

"I'm not ashamed of my uncle, Alma," he told her.

"No! Don't you dare bring him into this!" She clasped her hands convulsively. "It would be better to pay. Besides, you never could find him in time. We've not seen him for more than nine years."

"In some ways, Uncle Isaiah is a remarkable man, Alma."

"Remarkable! That's putting it gently. Oh, whatever possessed Costa's gang to come after us?" She wanted no more talk of Uncle Isaiah, it was clear. "They used to let decent people alone; or, anyway, they only plagued the foreigners and the colored folks."

"Costa's rising in society," Kinnaird observed with a wry little smile, "and we're not exempt any longer. Decent people don't count nowadays. Is the chief of police decent? Is the mayor decent? Costa, or Costa's friends, delivered the vote of this ward. Costa stands for democracy in action, *à la* North End."

"Then there's nowhere to appeal," she muttered, rising from her chair. "We'll pay."

Kinnaird motioned her back. "We'll appeal to Uncle Isaiah."

She gritted her teeth. "Appeal to a lunatic?"

"Isaiah was in the asylum for only two months—you know that."

"Yes, and I know that he escaped, and after he came out of hiding, his lawyers got him declared sane again. 'Homicide by reason of temporary insanity'—and so he never paid for the thing he had done that time, or for anything else of the sort. Oh, I know every old family has its nasty uncles, old men that play the fiddle and get drunk and never repay loans; I wouldn't much mind a man like that. But your famous Uncle Isaiah! Ugh, he's cold, cold, like a moccasin, and he's always watching. Whenever he came into a room, I shivered."

"Why, I thought he always was polite to you, Alma."

"Of course he was. His manners were exquisite, with everyone, and he dressed beautifully"—here she glanced caustically at her husband—"and he was clean as a scrubbed baby, and as rosy. 'But O! he was perfectly lovely to see, the pirate Dowdirk of Dundee.' You Kinnairds! I could see that Isaiah standing beside the stakes, watching witches burn—only he was born too late for that fun. You Scotch Kinnairds, with your cruel Old Testament names and your brimstone souls! You're scary enough, most of you; but Isaiah scared the wits out of his own family. You were frightened to death of him yourself, Daniel—you know you were."

Daniel winced, and then chuckled slightly. "Remember,

Alma, how when he was in a good humor he'd act Giant Despair? You lived just down the block, and you'd be over to play . . ."

"Do you think I'd forget? I lost five years' growth from that game. We'd be Christian and Faithful; then that dreadful Isaiah would come stealing up, in some sort of enormous black sack, and all of a sudden he'd pounce, and have us, and throw us in a closet. Oh, his cold hands, his long nails! I used to cry at night, after a day of that game; but I never dared refuse to play, because then perhaps Isaiah might have lost his good humor. How I hated him! I thought he was like a pet snake, that had to be fed on milk, and stroked, or he'd choke you."

"Really, Alma, you exaggerate. Uncle Isaiah wasn't warm hearted; but sometimes I loved him, and he knew it. He was charitable, too, and he never was in serious trouble with the city police, except for that affair before he went to the asylum."

"No," Alma interrupted, "usually it was the League of Nations that wanted to put him behind bars. I'll admit he had commercial talents. Smuggled guns, illegal immigrants and emigrants, opium . . ."

"After all, the opium was only for his own use, or perhaps for those Chinese and Indian friends of his, the mystics one used to find him with. Many times I was proud of him. He was eccentric in the grand manner, when all's said. Oh, there was an anarchic streak in him. But you've no cause to despise him so; and if anyone can help us now, it's Uncle Isaiah. Whatever he was or wasn't, he took a great pride in family, Alma. He'd send help or bring it, if he knew."

"Despise Isaiah? No, not that—I loathe him. Twice you

and I saw him in those trances, huddled in his chair like a dead man; you could have pushed a pin into him, and he'd not have stirred till his appointed time. That's what those opium-smoking 'mystic' freaks he patronized got him into. 'Out of the body,' he told us afterward. Out of his *mind* he was, really. But there's no danger of his meddling in this trouble: Isaiah Kinnaird would be a dead pigeon if he set foot in this country, let alone this city. He's in Omsk, Tomsk, or Tobolsk—or, for all anybody knows, in Hell. And you'll not find one soul in town who could or would give you his address, Daniel; so we may as well pay Costa."

Her husband leaned upon the kitchen table, his chin between his hands. "I don't know that," he said, slowly and somewhat maliciously. "I don't know. How about the Greek?"

* * *

In Water Street, a little way from the ferry docks, stands the Ares Cafe, its back to the sluggish river, its face to that sullen and nocturnally silent road of warehouses, even the green and red neon of its sign suffocated by river fog. Flanked by two valetudinarian potted ferns, a large simulated ham on a platter took pride of place in the front window; and upon the plate-glass was lettered boldly, "Woodrow Wilson Argyropoulous, Prop. Tables for Ladies." Above the cafe, two grimy windows looked down from what might be a loft or an office, with a separate entrance leading upstairs from the street to this floor.

Only a man with high talent for observing small details would have made out a device just above this entrance: a diminutive mirror fixed upon a steel bracket, tilted at such an angle that anyone looking from the window above could see who was at his door. Mr. Isaiah Kinnaird had fastened that mirror in place, for his office had been over the Ares Cafe. It had mattered to Uncle Isaiah, Daniel Kinnaird reflected, that he should have a glimpse of his queer visitors before they got in. Now Daniel Kinnaird stood here by the Ares Cafe, looking through the plate-glass into the restaurant.

It being half-past nine in the evening the Greek had only one patron, finishing a cup of coffee, and the Greek was engaged in his old pastime of demonstrating his private solution of the riddle of the business cycle. Pencil in hand, sheets of paper on the counter by the coffee urn, he drew interminable circles and curves and triangles, gesticulating with his left arm, his voice drifting through the open doorway to Kinnaird.

"O.K., Mr. Bronkowski? You with me so far? O.K. Now the bank give me seventeen thousand more . . ."

A tiny boy emerged from behind the coffee urn and tugged masterfully at Argyropoulous: "Pencil, Papa, pencil."

"Go 'way, boy," sighed the Greek, benevolently. "Now, Mr. Bronkowski, this straight?" The customer agreed. Outside the window, Daniel Kinnaird shifted impatiently; he must get the Greek alone.

"Pencil, Papa, pencil!" the tiny boy demanded. In despair, the Greek surrendered his pencil. And at that moment, while still watching the scene within the cafe, Daniel Kinnaird came to feel that he himself was watched.

He turned in alarm. But no man was in the street, not Costa nor the squat man nor anyone else. Then his eyes caught the surface of the mirror above his head: reflected in it was a face, peering downward from the lightless window above the mirror. Though dim in what light came from the cafe sign, this face could be made out tolerably well. A small, square countenance, with deep lines at either side of the mouth, and topped by thick white hair. A civil, if somewhat sardonic, expression was on the firm lips; the large eyes were shadowed by tufted eyebrows. It was Mr. Isaiah Kinnaird. Next, this reflection was gone.

In astounded urgency, Daniel Kinnaird tugged at the door leading to the office above, but it was locked. To have cried out Uncle Isaiah's name would not have been prudent, he reminded himself, even in this frantic moment. Regardless of the solitary customer, Kinnaird burst into the cafe and said to the Greek, panting, "Woodie, I have to talk with you."

"Play with the pencil, boy," the Greek told his son, patting his head. Woodie's black eyes ran over Kinnaird's pale face. "You come in the kitchen, Mr. Kinnaird?" They went behind the swinging door, back by the sink. "You got troubles, Mr. Kinnaird?"

"My Uncle Isaiah's upstairs," said Daniel Kinnaird. "Take me up, Woodie."

The Greek scowled, blinked, and then laughed. "Ho! You joking, Mr. Kinnaird? Ho! You know I ain't seen your uncle for nine, ten years. Nobody seen him. Cuba, Mexico—who knows? Not here, never. Ho, ho! Not healthy in Water Street, not now."

"I saw him in the mirror, Woodie. He'll want to talk with me. Take me up."

The Greek's grin faded. "Christ A'mighty, Mr. Kinnaird,

you don't joke? You feel good? No, Mr. Kinnaird, by Christ A'mighty, your uncle ain't up there, nobody up there. Listen." He raised his hand. A screen slammed—it was the customer going out—and then they heard only the sound of the little boy scribbling in the cafe. From the office above, not the faintest rustle. Lowering his hand, "Nobody up there, not for years."

"Show me the way up, Woodie," Daniel Kinnaird insisted. "I've got to see my uncle. Costa's on my track."

"God damn to hell!" The Greek shrugged in vexation. "The truth, that's what I tell. O.K., come up, Mr. Kinnaird, if you got to." He took two keys from the knife drawer and led the way through the cafe to the outer door. "Costa," he added, very low. "Oh, bad. You pay, Mr. Kinnaird. *I* pay." They went outside, and the Greek unlocked the separate door opening upon the stairs, and they ascended some steep black steps. Then another door stopped them; the Greek had some trouble with the lock of this one. After fumbling, he got it open, and they were in a big dark loft of a place.

"No electric lights, Mr. Kinnaird," said the Greek—or rather, he whispered it. Dim shapes of furniture loomed up: a desk, some sort of long counter, a safe, a table, three or four elderly chairs, a filing cabinet. The shadows at the far end were extremely thick.

"How about a flashlight, Woodie?" Shaking his head, the Greek felt along the counter, and presently had a candle in his hand; he lit it. No, those shadows were shadows only. Beyond the place where they had been, two more windows looked upon the river, a door between them. "Show me what's on the other side of that door, Woodie." The Greek fitted a key to it, and when it creaked open they looked upon the oily river. They stood high above the water; a rickety flight of steps, supported by piers, twisted down to the quay and the mouth of an alley. With now and then a gurgle or hiss, the tide was slipping languidly out. "All right, Woodie," said Daniel Kinnaird, "I apologize to you. Fancies, fancies."

Closing the river door, they stood in the middle of the disused office. "What the hell," the Greek said, "I know. Me, I want him back, too, Mr. Kinnaird. You think about him coming, maybe, and think, and after while you hear steps outside, and you say, 'Christ A'mighty, that's Isaiah Kinnaird!' Ho! Nothing there. Your uncle, he's too smart to come back, ever. Mexico, Cuba, Brazil, who knows? But not here. If he was, then no Costa, hey? No Costa? Your uncle, he don't spit on Costa, hey?"

"Why didn't you rent this place afterward, Woodie?"

The Greek ran his hand through his scanty hair. "I get no money for this dump, Mr. Kinnaird. And your uncle, he lend me money. And he take me up here sometimes, me and my first boy, and we talk. Oh, how your uncle talk, Mr. Kinnaird! What a friend, so good! What he don't know, Christ A'mighty, it don't matter a damn. And he make funny poems to tickle my first boy, like this:

> " 'Woodrow Wilson Argyropoulous,
>   Born to rule this grand metropolis . . .'

"No, I leave things like he had 'em. If your uncle crazy, Mr. Kinnaird, I like every guy in Water Street crazy. Smart! No, I leave things like he had 'em. 'Woodrow,' your uncle say, 'Woodrow, I put my trust in you.' Kind! Oh, Christ A'mighty, a good man. I leave things like you see."

"Woodie," Kinnaird asked, "isn't there a chance *someone* knows where to reach my uncle?"

"All right," the Greek said. "All right. One guy you try. What the hell, you try him. The lawyer, Simmich. Your uncle, Simmich did stuff for him." Woodie led the way back down the stairs and into the cafe, and there scribbled an address on the back of an old menu. "He don't know; but you try him." Opening the door, the Greek started to speak again, hesitated as if doubting his discretion, and then muttered, "You know your uncle, he usta pray?"

"I never thought of him as pious."

"Oh, Mr. Kinnaird, sure. Pray? Christ A'mighty, he talk low when he talk with you; but when he pray—maybe I wash dishes down here, and I hear him pray loud, loud, hear him through the ceiling. Your uncle, he pray to God to choke his enemies. And it come true, Mr. Kinnaird, it come true every time. Oh, a good man. But me and you, we got to deal with Costa. Best to pay. Sorry, Mr. Kinnaird. So long."

As he left, Kinnaird took a surreptitious glance at the mirror overhead, but of course it was blank. Simmich lived within walking distance; and though the hour was past eleven, Kinnaird couldn't wait until morning. He came to an old brick flat-building on the edge of a slum-clearance project, took the automatic elevator up four flights, found a door with a plate engraved "D. L. Simmich, Attorney," and rang the bell. After two more rings, a thin fellow with nasty little eyes, in slippers and shirtsleeves, opened the door. "Well?"

"My name is Kinnaird."

Simmich's manner altered; he peered into the hall, either way. "Come in, please, Mr. Kinnaird." They sat in a living room with walls of a dirty cream, and Simmich said, "Related to *him?*"

"I need to get in touch with my uncle immediately. What can you do about it?"

The nasty eyes roved calculatingly over Kinnaird's mild face and shabby suit. "I play my hand straight, Mr. Kinnaird. I haven't had word of Isaiah Kinnaird for three years. But it might be possible to inquire among some—among certain foreign associates of Mr. Kinnaird's. Just possible, understand. Of course, there'd be cablegrams, and registry fees, and my ordinary charges . . ."

"Go ahead," Kinnaird told him. "I take it that my uncle's transactions with you turned out satisfactorily, Mr. Simmich."

"Oh, yes; prompt and agreeable, your uncle, even though fixed in his opinions." The nasty eyes seemed to recalculate possible extortion against possible retribution. Simmich sighed slightly. "The costs won't be prohibitive, Mr. Kinnaird. I'll commence first thing in the morning."

"Begin by cable, please, tonight." With some inner reluctance, Daniel Kinnaird shook hands with Simmich, and went down to the foggy road, and turned into Water Street, as good a way home as any. Even cables could hardly be expeditious enough. Uncle Isaiah left his brand on people.

* * *

Well past midnight, alone in Water Street with his worries, Kinnaird again approached the Ares Cafe. Now the cafe was unlighted, the Greek having closed when Kinnaird left and gone down the block to his four rooms and seven dependents. Daniel Kinnaird could recall, fragmentarily, having spent hours, when he was on vacation from school, in that dusty office above the cafe—hours of a fearful joy spent on a stool beside his impenetrable Uncle Isaiah, shuffling bundles of old invoices, and now and then daring to tease Uncle Isaiah into some game. Small and straight and impeccably neat, his uncle never had been out of temper, never had seemed in the least busy; and his skin had been tight and smooth as a very young man's. But you did not take liberties. His mother, Daniel Kinnaird realized later, had not much liked his hours in that office; but she never had ventured to put her objections into words. If you knew Uncle Isaiah, you rarely risked talking about him, no matter how many walls separated you from him; for he knew, he *knew*.

Amidst these recollected images, Daniel Kinnaird walked slowly past the Ares Cafe, when a sensation made him stop short. For the past two or three seconds, an odor had drifted faintly about his nose; and now that odor found its cubby in his memory. It was the scent of a soap; it was the odor of the delicate and costly soap that Uncle Isaiah had used, the smell which always emanated from Uncle Isaiah's white shirts and square small self, the aroma of an old-fashioned man's soap. And an odor it was, no mere memory.

Daniel Kinnaird, swinging about, leaped toward the doorway of the cafe. No one was in that doorway nor in the adjacent recess of the door to the office; but someone must have been there not more than half a minute before. For the second time that night, Kinnaird tugged at the door which led upstairs, and now it yielded. In he went, up the steps, treading on his toes so as to hear any sound above him.

And before he had gone up six treads, a sound did come from somewhere at the stairhead: a whistle, infinitely soft, but a whistled tune, "Dixie." After a few more seconds, during which Kinnaird felt the hair rising along the back of his neck, the whistle gave way to a low humming, and then distinct words, sung in a melodious deep voice, though muffled:

> " 'There'll be buckwheat cakes and Injun batter,
>   Make you fat or a little fatter,
> Look away, look away, look away, Dixie land.' "

"Uncle Isaiah!" called Kinnaird. How well he knew voice and tune! "Isaiah Kinnaird!" In three bounds, Daniel Kinnaird was at the top of the staircase and shoving against the door. But it would not budge.

Now the chant had ceased. Kinnaird rattled the knob, tried to force the bolt. "Uncle Isaiah!" For he felt something stirring on the other side of the door. "It's been nine years, Uncle Isaiah!" To his mind's eye came a vision of the man behind that warped door: Mr. Isaiah Kinnaird, ageless, with his peculiar jaunty dignity, his aloof whistling, his stiff collars, his faint scent of soap, his good dark clothes, his stout thorn walking stick, his square, genteel, old-young face with the tufted eyebrows and the restless eyes of a light blue. "Uncle Isaiah!"

After this last cry, silence fell for a whole minute; then a quiet voice said, somewhere inside the loft, "Good evening to you, Daniel, from your bad mad old uncle."

"Let me in, Uncle Isaiah." No reply, but some noise like the scratching of a stick upon the floor. "Uncle, are you ill?"

Now Isaiah Kinnaird's voice rang clearer and stronger, full of his old whimsical deliberation. "In me, Daniel, decades of celibacy and sobriety are rewarded. I'm as hearty as I was when last we met. But if you will pardon my recurrent eccentricity, we will keep this door shut."

"I've got something urgent to discuss with you, Uncle, and it's been nine years since we were together, you know."

"I'm aware of both facts, Daniel, my nephew; yet you will understand that I am here on sufferance; my tenure is precarious; and my present arrangements require that our intercourse take place wholly *per vox*, however undignified this may seem to you." There was a deep chuckle.

"Uncle," said Daniel Kinnaird, his heart warming, "come home with me. It's dark, and you won't be seen. I need your help. Incidentally, your landlord, Mr. Argyropolous, is a consummate liar."

"We Kinnairds shouldn't sit in judgment so summarily, Daniel. Although Woodrow bears some affection for me, I think my presence might embarrass him just now, and he has no notion I am here.

> 'Thus sang the jolly miller, upon the banks of Dee:
> I care for nobody, no not I, and nobody cares for me.'

"Whenever I have deviated from this principle, Daniel, I have suffered. You recall, too, the injunction of our Stoic preceptor, 'Live as if upon a mountain.' This affair of yours which I'm to settle requires especial privacy."

"What am I to do, Uncle?" Daniel Kinnaird was resigned

now to conducting this extraordinary interview through a locked door: it never had been of any avail to oppose the whims of Uncle Isaiah.

"As for coming home with you," Uncle Isaiah went on, "why, candidly—I fear Alma wouldn't survive the shock without some preparation, eh? Besides, my scheme requires you to keep all this from Alma—which shouldn't be really difficult for you, given our family's congenital proclivity to secrecy. Well, now, to business. I understand that you are in difficulty with a certain Bruno Costa."

"People like that never dared trouble us before, Uncle."

"Right, and therefore our dismissal of him should be rather curt, eh? Mr. Costa scarcely understands our family, Daniel. But in any case, I suspect Costa's necessities force him to seek revenue from sources normally left unmolested. Formerly, I understand, Costa confined his exactions to persons who could not speak three consecutive sentences of proper English, and so were bubbles in this great melting pot of ours. But he must have spent a peck of money to get his pardon in company so august, and he's endeavoring to recoup his losses—indeed, to fulfill certain promises. Well, we must rebuff him, Daniel, my nephew."

"And how?"

"Listen to me: offer Costa's agent a lump-sum settlement, rather than weekly payments; and insist upon a personal interview with Mr. Costa."

"But could we trust Costa to keep away, after he'd got his lump sum?"

"Naturally not. Our offer is bait, Daniel, to bring him to the interview. That meeting will be conducted right here, tomorrow night, at half-past eleven; and I'm the one who'll clean Mr. Costa's clock for him. Tell his man that Mr. Kinnaird wants to talk with Costa. You needn't mention which Kinnaird."

"What can you arrange, Uncle Isaiah?" Mr. Isaiah Kinnaird, his nephew reflected, was a gentleman remarkably versatile; but he was Lord knows how old, and Daniel Kinnaird did not quite relish the idea of leaving him alone with a hoodlum like Costa.

"Daniel, I ought not to have to tell you that I don't tolerate inquiries into my business procedures. I'll solve your problem for you: that's enough. And since I am sedulous not to attract attention from Woodrow or anyone else, will you leave me to my lucubrations? Costa's to come here at eleven-thirty tomorrow, remember." There was some relish in the voice.

"When shall we meet, Uncle?" Daniel Kinnaird felt a thorough fool, separated from his nearest kinsman, after nine years, by an inch of pine.

"That, Daniel boy, is in the dispensation of a merciful Providence, and hangs also upon the issue of our business tomorrow night. Goodbye, Daniel." Perfect silence followed on the other side of the panel. And Kinnaird, knowing the futility of crossing his uncle, went reluctantly down the stairs and across the street.

No light showed at the upper windows: elusive as a bat or a nightbird, Isaiah Kinnaird. His nephew shivered for a moment, and then hurried home, half dazed, but reassured.

* * *

To his wife, at breakfast, Kinnaird said nothing but that he had no intention of paying Costa, and would therefore "make other arrangements." He ignored her frightened exasperation. All day he was fairly cheerful; and at closing time, again, the squat man entered Kinnaird's Cleaners.

"Cough up the dues, brother," said the squat man, from the corner of his mouth.

"I'd rather make a final settlement with Mr. Costa," Kinnaird told him.

Speculatively the squat man chewed a cigar. "That's up to the boss."

"Then I'll meet him at eleven-thirty tonight, over the Ares Cafe, Water Street." Kinnaird was firm about it; the squat man looked taken aback.

"The boss makes the dates, see," he said.

"If Costa wants a cash settlement, he'll be there, my friend."

"O.K., O.K.," the squat man agreed, almost plaintive; "but if you get the boss riled, it's your funeral. Say, you ain't plannin' any cute stuff?" He stared again at Kinnaird's mild face. "No, I guess you wouldn't." And he went away.

Kinnaird locked the shop and ate a hearty supper. "You Kinnairds!" Alma said to him. "What have you done? Sometimes you're as clammy as your uncle."

Selecting a book, Daniel Kinnaird settled himself in a corner by the grandfather clock.

* * *

About half-past eleven that night, a tall and swarthy man emerged from an alley on the north side of Water Street and crossed toward the Ares Cafe. He wore an expensive suit of loud check, and he walked with a swagger, throwing his shoulders back, glancing challengingly from under the brim of his low-crowned hat. There was no one to challenge. He tried the door to the office above the cafe, found it unlocked, and felt for a light switch: none could be discovered. So he mounted the stairs in darkness, and knocked at the upper door. No one answered. With a curse, he pushed it open and slipped inside.

Upon a naked table in the middle of the long, dusty room, a single candle was burning. Shadows half hid the farther end of the loft, but he could make out a door there, and he could see no one waiting for him. "Kinnaird?" he grunted.

Then—did it come from behind that old safe?—Costa heard a soft humming, as if some one were trying variations on a sea-chanty. In a deep voice, someone was crooning—

"I'd a Bible in my hand when I sailed, when I sailed;
I'd a Bible in my hand when I sailed.
I'd a Bible in my hand by my father's great command,
But I sunk it in the sand when I sailed."

"Kinnaird, that you?" Rather than replying, the deep voice repeated the chorus, placidly, drawling out "by my father's great command," and then ending with abrupt speed, "But I sunk it in the sand when I sailed."

Still no one appeared. "Kinnaird!" Costa demanded. He closed the door behind him. When it went shut, there occurred a distinct click. Costa started. Keeping his face to the room, he felt at the back of him with his left hand, seeking the knob, while he slid his right hand cautiously into a coat pocket. There was no knob; there was no internal lock; the door, so far as he could tell, was secured by some hidden spring. "Kinnaird!" Costa called, furious.

Did something shift, over there by the other door, out from behind the safe? Now a voice said, in a mere murmur, "Mr. Bruno Costa, I see." Costa crouched instinctively.

"You playin' games, Kinnaird? Come on out!" In Costa's voice was a nervous shrillness.

Then someone did come from the shadows, moving into the dim aura of light on the far side of the candle. It was a self-assured old man, small but squarely built, dressed with care; he played with a good walking stick; his head was bare, and in the flicker of the candle Costa could see that he had thick white hair, a fresh pink skin, and great eyebrows that made his eyes circles of shadow. "What the hell!" cried Costa. "Who're you?"

"I represent Mr. Daniel Kinnaird," said the old gentleman, composedly. "My name is Isaiah Kinnaird. We haven't met previously, Mr. Costa. I'm here to arrange a final settlement with you." He smiled courteously.

"Yeah?" Costa hesitated, and knew that the old man perceived his incertitude; so he strode defiantly to the middle of the room, where he stared across the table at the old man. Costa kept his hand in his pocket. "Yeah? No, we ain't met, but I heard about you, you crazy old bastard. What's up?"

"I look upon you, sir," said Isaiah Kinnaird, "as an interesting phenomenon of social disintegration, a representative specimen of these depraved days. Your reference to my origin is inaccurate; for only one instance of illegitimacy has been recorded among the Kinnairds in more than a century; while you, Mr. Costa—if you will forgive my saying so—manifestly are the end-product of many generations of unbridled lubricity."

"Cut the comedy," Costa snarled, grimacing in a way

that should have been alarming. "Are you and that pants-presser going to ante?"

Now old Kinnaird came still closer to the table, so that the candle showed him very plain, and Costa could see his eyes. They were blue, and would have been innocent, had they not slid and rolled so wildly. "Jesus!" Costa gasped, a lump in his throat, "I don't do business with nobody that's bughouse."

"Costa," Mr. Kinnaird resumed, politely smiling, "I believe we shall make our final settlement now. You were imprudent this night. Surely you noticed how that door locked behind you?"

"Keep away," Costa spat out, shifting his hand in his pocket. "You going to ante?"

"Are you in tolerable health, Mr. Costa?" Having said this, the old man rapidly slipped one of his slender hands (in this instant, Costa saw how terribly long the nails were) across the dusty table, and touched Costa upon the wrist. Yelling, Costa sprang to one side.

"Oh God! Keep them hands off me!" Isaiah Kinnaird was sidling round the table. "Keep away, you old bastard!" And now Costa pulled his automatic; but Kinnaird's white hand was quicker; and as its fingers touched Costa's, the tall man screamed again, and the gun fell under the table.

What followed might have been ludicrous to anyone that witnessed it. A powerful man, in the prime of life, dodged and ducked about the room, vaulting the table, scampering past the desk, for an instant seeking sanctuary behind the safe, trying always to gain the back door. Now and again he shrieked as his pursuer nearly grasped him. Always in his way, intercepting, snatching, chuckling, darted a small elderly man, his white hair disordered, his eyes alight, his veined hands extended, one gripping a stick.

Then Costa saw an opening: he doubled back, rolled under the table, and ran straight for the door to the river. But just before he could reach it, his foot touched the rung of a chair, and he went to his knees. Almost in the same moment he rose; yet as he caught his balance, Isaiah Kinnaird protruded his stick, tripped Costa, and was upon him.

* * *

When the clock struck midnight, Daniel Kinnaird put down his book. By now, the conference in Water Street should be concluded; and his uncle would have warned Costa off. At the last stroke of the clock, however, an engulfing conviction burst upon Daniel Kinnaird—something that devastated the marches of ordinary perception. He thought he heard a man's shriek and a chuckle anciently familiar, associated in his memory with a great black sack. All this invaded his consciousness as if someone had tumbled him into a freezing pool.

Who knows the whole power of passionate entreaty, or what a desperate longing may conjure from the depths? Into Kinnaird's bewildered mind flashed a dozen curious sensations of the past evening: the scent of soap, the tune of "Dixie"; and without snatching up hat or coat, he ran out of his door into the road, and through the paper-littered ways of the North End toward Water Street. Some things even a Costa ought not to face.

From the pavement, he could see an insufficient light flicker behind the drawn shades of the office above the Ares Cafe. His flesh creeping, Daniel Kinnaird climbed the stairs and pulled open the door at the top. A candle, almost wholly guttered, allowed him to inspect an empty loft. One chair had been overturned; something had brushed dust from the table top. That back door to the river stairs stood ajar, creaking intermittently in the breeze.

Daniel Kinnaird went upon the crazy platform, and heard the tide sucking at ooze, and saw some bird of night flap over the water toward the soiled and decrepit streets of the North End. But of Isaiah Kinnaird, or of Bruno Costa, no trace—not that night, nor the next day, nor ever.

OFF THE SAND ROAD

♤

The old road had slouched through a cedar swamp, where mosquitoes hovered thick as fog over pools almost level with the track; but now the doctor and the two Bass boys came out upon a barren, fringed by silent woods. Ragged stumps, patches of brown rot contrasting with their naked gray sides, stretched for a mile across rolling country, and then scrub oak and second-growth pine closed the view. This land, nothing but sand held down by desperate clumps of grass, was unfenced, though a lopsided sign proclaimed "No Trasepsing." Under the July sun the scrawled sign was fading toward obliteration.

The only other mark of possession was a roofless log cabin; and a side trail, fainter even than the old road, showed no mark of wheels. "They're thick in here, Doc-

tor," said Harry, the older Bass boy; and the three of them, swinging their pails, turned down the side trail toward a cluster of wild strawberry plants.

Sand flowed from the forlorn ruts into their shoes; sometimes they sank in it nearly to their ankles. The doctor, on vacation from Chicago, ate nearly as many of the small berries as he dropped into his pail, but the Bass boys—Frank, nine years old, and his brother, fourteen—picked swiftly and earnestly, being native to the land: obtaining a tolerable livelihood in Pottawattomie County required frugality and diligence.

The sun burned the doctor's urban neck, deerflies plagued him as they approached the woods, and he longed for a drink in this cut-over desert. Harry and Frank picked on, though, so that presently the three worked near to the northern side of the barren. And now the doctor noticed a farmstead tucked into a hollow around a bend of the sand road: little house, shed, and shingled barn, all so weathered that they seemed as much a part of the ravaged barren as the stumps which hemmed them in.

"Whose place is that, boys?" the doctor asked, by way of diversion.

"That's where Mr. Clatry lived, Doctor Cross," said Frank, in the conspicuously proper English the consolidated school instilled into country children these days. "Want to see it?"

"Is the house empty?" The doors, he could make out, were shut, and there was glass in the windows, and the place looked more nearly habitable than some of the tar-paper shacks of the sand-hill farmers he had seen earlier in the week. A high-pitched roof shadowed walls of what seemed to be either stone or some sort of concrete block, although the bulk of a giant lonely sycamore kept the doctor from having a clear view.

"Nobody's stayed there since Mrs. Clatry went away two summers ago," Frank answered in his eager little voice. "The man that owns it now lives in Detroit, and he can't get anybody to rent. It's bad land, anyway. We can make a short cut across the field."

"Is this a field?" the doctor muttered, mostly to himself, for it was bad land indeed. Indian paintbrush, sweet fern, and milkweed brushed the doctor's ankles, and the soil was lucky to support even these plants; for where vegetation was gone altogether, the wind and the spring rains created little Saharas, some of them fifty to a hundred yards wide, miniature dunes and troughs of a coarse yellow sand which stirred and shifted, even on so quiet a day as this, like sleepy animate terrors.

"What could they raise?"

"Corn," said Harry, moderately proud of his intimacy with the economy of Pottawattomie, "and beans and potatoes. Anyway, they tried. Dad says some folks can raise corn in this blow-sand, and some can't. Nobody ever did well here. Years ago a man bought this place at a tax sale, for sixty-eight dollars. But he wasn't able to rent it until Mr. Clatry came." Harry was expertly dismembering a grasshopper he had caught, manifesting the inoffensive savagery of boys on easy terms with nature.

"Ma never let us go here before, Doctor," Frank interjected. "But I don't think she'll mind with you along. Nothing's going to get us if you're around. She said she'd tan us if we fussed with that old well." He nodded toward the steel windmill, now close.

"That looks like a new derrick," remarked the doctor. The metal glistened repulsively against the somber tones of the barren.

"That man in Detroit had it put up when Mr. Clatry came to stay," Harry commented. "I bet he's sorry now. Dad says Mr. Clatry couldn't have really meant to farm the place; probably he figured he'd get along on a garden and jobs in town. The Clatrys didn't have a Ford or anything, so Mr. Clatry walked in every day, when there was work. He didn't get much. He couldn't lift heavy things, because he was hurt in the war. He was almost forty, but he'd been in the Pacific fighting for years, and had medals. Maybe they'd have got along on his pension, all the same, if Mrs. Clatry hadn't had all those kids."

The house was built of a curious homemade mortar block, the doctor could see now, though the barn and the shed were log. At the two front windows, dingy yellow shades were pulled part way down. Many houses have the faces of animals, and this one seemed to whine like a stupid old dog. Cheap and rusty, a padlock secured the door. "Let's try the side, Doctor," Frank shrilled, trotting round to the slanting cellar door. Harry pulled it open, and the dank smell of bare earth drifted up; they descended the few steps. Some sacks of fertilizer, a hoe, a snapped saw, mason jars—these and a mess of trifles littered the place. No stair led from the cellar to the house above, so they withdrew to the daylight.

"Didn't they take anything with them?" The doctor was gingerly climbing the rickety back stoop.

"Oh, Mrs. Clatry had funny ways," Harry said. "When she got a mood on, she wouldn't stop for hell or high water." Frank chuckled.

"I don't like to poke around, boys, without . . ." But as he spoke, the back door yielded sulkily to his pressure, and they were in a rough kitchen swarming with flies. Torn papers, smashed food jars, and the amorphous filth which always finds its way to the floors of gutted houses made entering a delicate process. The doctor picked his way past a wood stove to open an inner door.

"The kids took after her," observed Frank. "They used to beat the dickens out of littler boys at school. They had white hair, Doctor, all five. They were fat, but Mr. Clatry was thin. Dad says they worried Mr. Clatry to a frazzle. They weren't his kids: Mrs. Clatry had them before she married Mr. Clatry."

One bare-walled room and an alcove on the east side: this was all the lower floor of the house, except for the kitchen. The square room, with an unrailed staircase opposite the front door, was full of furniture; and the furniture was knocked topsy-turvy, much of it smashed—old straight chairs from secondhand shops and tawdry late-Victorian sofa and heavy table, with its blue paint flaking. Someone, perhaps a gang of youngsters, had preceded them to the Clatry house. But the contents must have been nearly worthless. Movie magazines and confessions-pulps had been ripped apart and strewn everywhere. At the foot of the stairway, a bunch of evangelical tracts sprawled forlornly.

"Do you know who she is?" The doctor had picked up a snapshot which lay beside a battered Bible. A heavy woman in her middle thirties, not unhandsome, looked toward the boys—her eyes wide, her full lips held in an uncertain smile. As if she had moved nervously, her arm blurred the lower half of the photograph.

"That's Mrs. Clatry. See the white building behind her, Doctor? It's the Followers of God church. Mrs. Clatry used to walk to the main road and hitchhike to the Followers of God meeting every Sunday, Ma says." Frank manipulated a yo-yo he had found in an orange crate. Well, thought the doctor, that explains the tracts by the stairs.

Presently, disregarding the bad list of the steps, the boys scrambled to the loft. "Look at the letters, Doctor!" By the time the doctor had made his way up, Harry was tearing stamps off old envelopes for his album. A cardboard carton of correspondence, once tied with a blue ribbon that now trailed across broken bedsprings, had been hurled across the low room, spilling most of its contents; but the letters lay on the floor like a dropped deck of cards, and as the doctor idly picked them up, he found they were roughly in chronological order. In this loft, too, everything was battered and mutilated. He pushed aside a chest of drawers lacking its knobs, a child's hideous iron bed, a bushel basket of cheap dishes. Though this place was hot, the doctor shuffled the bunch of letters while the boys hunted their stamps.

She wrote a hand legible enough, this Mrs. Ella Clatry, and orthographical blunders were infrequent. Here was a letter in red ink, apparently the earliest of the lot; it protruded from a stained envelope addressed to a Corporal Gerald Clatry, at a San Francisco APO. "What was Mr. Clatry's first name?" asked the doctor.

The boys conferred. "Gerald, I guess," Harry said. They

were prying out the dresser drawers now. The doctor leaned against the bedsprings and read:

"Dearest Jerry,

"Tho't I would try and write you again tonight. You've been writing to me *every* night, so I should write to you that often if possible. And, besides, I need someone kind and understanding to talk to!

"Hope you can read my writing all right. Ralph seemed to object to my using his typewriter, even tho' he told me I could use it whenever I wanted to; so I got me some more stationery and some new penpoints and a bottle of ink tonight. I don't like red ink as well as I do green, but it is better than those terrible dark colors, and I couldn't get any green or violet.

"My! I'm so sleepy and tired, Jerry, that I can scarcely see to write! I've *got* to do it, tho', for you. The things you have to face over there must be terrible, but nevertheless I believe I'd rather be there, with you, than here. At least, I'd have somebody nice to talk to, and I'd just as soon have bombs and bullets coming at me, as some of the things that have been coming my way lately, Jerry. I sure have you to thank for those lovely letters you have written me. They are about the only pleasant things of any kind that have come my way for the last month! In other words, they have been the only sweetness in my bitter cup! I *need your letters* as bad as you do mine! At a time when all my plans seemed to go wrong, and all my 'so called' friends failed me, somehow, the Lord in His mercy saw fit to give me a friend away across the ocean! Maybe it is best that way. If you are not a true friend I won't be so apt to find it out, at least not so soon. *Please*, Jerry, my friend, forgive me for feeling that way about it! But it has been proven to me, more than once, that the only *really true* 'friend' that one has is The Lord!

"Last night I felt so very weary and tired of everything in this earthly life! I wish I had your shoulder to cry on (but maybe you wouldn't like that). Anyway, I'm sure it's best the way it is! I can cry it out, on my knees, and tell *Him* all about it!

"Think I'll go to sleep now, if I can. Goodnight, Jerry.

"Love,

"Ella"

Among the letters, the doctor noticed several postal money-order applications, completed but never submitted, drawn in favor of two firms of tract-publishers. Thrust among them were notations of tract-titles: "Brooks in the Wilderness"; "Sins Eradicated." There was another blank with the name of a firm quite different upon it, pinned to a coupon requesting a copy of "Intelligent Sex Relations." He found a second letter in red ink, written a week before the first; in this Ella recounted a long tale of tribulation—disobedient children, boredom, unending work about the house. She was living with relatives, it appeared—some cousin who was married to Clatry's sister Jane. Her former husband was paying her alimony to the amount of twenty-one dollars a month, which she was expected to contribute wholly to the household's expenses. She didn't think it was right. Here an interruption occurred: "Maybe I can resume my writing again now, after having to go upstairs and use a belt on some very disobedient youngsters." The sun hadn't shone for days. And Ralph and Jane expected her to do all the work. "I hope and pray that the Lord will provide a way for me to get out of it before long!" She listened to John Wellam and his "Nation Back to Faith" program on the radio every Sunday. Did Jerry hear it overseas? She hoped so.

The doctor recognized a querulousness close to hysteria,

as clearly as if the woman had stood before him. He glanced over the concluding sheet of the letter:

"I wonder if Jane was right when she told me I was just 'wasting my time' writing to you? And when I said I was beginning to like you, she said I was 'riding for a fall.' Maybe I should take her advice and not only quit writing to you, but also refuse to read your letters!

"I wonder why it is, that because of the circumstances brought on by past sins, and mistakes, that one must 'exclude' *all* the sweetness in the present, and all 'hope' for any happiness in the *future?* Must one go on paying and paying until the end of time? You can thank God, Jerry, that you have been fortunate enough never to have got yourself mixed up in matrimony! You don't have to worry about a broken home and several little children plus a divorce!

"Well, I sent the children to Sunday school this morning, but I didn't go. I should have, I suppose, but the minister's wife over here in the church appears to be entirely lacking in Charity toward others. Seems to think she's 'perfect' and expects everybody else to be the same way. I don't mean to criticize, but she really gets under my skin."

Scowling, the doctor dropped this letter and leafed through an accumulation of bills, statements, and duns. "Was Mr. Clatry good to the children?"

"He was a real nice, quiet man," Frank answered from the middle of a pile of old clothes.

"He had to be good to them, or they'd of kicked him in the creek," added Harry. "They were some peelers. He was a lot better to them than Mrs. Clatry was. One day Jimmy Clatry came to school and there was a big red burn on his neck, and the teacher asked him how he got it. He said his Ma poured scalding water on him because he dropped his plate."

But she wrote verse, it appeared. Indeed, there was a letter trying to sell lyrics to a music publisher—never mailed, like those money orders; and here was something she had sent to Gerald Clatry:

"I wrote this the day after I wrote *A Gentleman Speaks His Mind, A Proposal*. It gave me the inspiration for the other one.

> "If you and I lived all alone
> In this here place that we call home,
> I s'pose you'd keep me on the run,
> But sure, and we'd have lots of fun!"

Pinned to this effort was a clipping from an Ohio weekly: "Married Friday, March 7, Ella Fowler and Gerald Clatry. Mr. Clatry's mother and two sisters and niece from Ulysses were present. Mr. Clatry, who spent four years with the Army in the South Pacific, was recently released from Bushnell General Hospital."

"Did your folks know the Clatrys well?" the doctor inquired.

"Nobody saw much of Mr. and Mrs. Clatry," Harry told him. "It's too far out of the beaten track, this place. They weren't good mixers, anyway."

"Some days nobody came by here at all," Frank added. He dug up a soiled garrison cap from among the old clothes. "About the only folks that use the sand road are the Whittakers, when they're walking and want to take a short cut. Or sometimes people come out this way to Lost Lake, where the fishing's only fair, and the brush has got awful high."

"Look at the bills!" said Harry, as the doctor dropped half a handful of them to the plank floor. "Ma says Mrs. Clatry used to come in the drugstore and buy Hollywood magazines by the armload, the kids tagging along behind her, with dirty faces. Not that they had money. They ended up owing all the stores. Mrs. Clatry told people she just couldn't help herself when she got in a dime store—she had to bring home all the new things to try out. Mr. Clatry was different, but they say after a while he stopped arguing with her about buying junk, because he only got himself in Dutch. She sure could fly off the handle. One day Pat Whittaker was walking along the road and he heard a yelling and there was Mrs. Clatry chasing Mr. Clatry round and round the barn with a rake, hitting him when she could. She was a big woman. Mr. Clatry took it; he didn't want to fight any more. Another time, some men from the city, hunting, went past here toward Lost Lake, and later they asked Dad, 'What goes on at that dump up the sand road? The woman was after the man with an axe, right out in the yard. He grabbed it away from her, and threw it in the grass, and dodged into the house, and she went in after him.'"

She had bought novelties by mail, too. The doctor came upon a bill for "two live male hamsters and two live female hamsters, shipped by Railway Express." An artificial-flowers-material firm asked payment for "covered wire, cloth lilies of the valley, wool fibre." She had toyed with correspondence courses, one in "artistic lettering." And presently she had come to begging—at first by implication, later without hesitation. A well-known national charity wrote that her case was not within their jurisdiction. A couple in Colorado replied: "Sorry things are working so badly for you, but don't know what we can do." Mrs. Clatry had better luck with a Grand Rapids woman, who sent a Christmas card: "I'm the one you met in the toy department, remember? I hope this small gift of money will help make a happier Christmas for you and your family."

Frank had discovered some corporal's chevrons and was displaying them against his sleeve. "Once she told Mrs. Collins," he remarked, "that she simply *had* to buy things to keep her mind off the sand on the ridge. The sand got into her frying-pan when she was cooking supper; it was always coming through the window sills and into the beds. And nobody ever came to talk to her. She thought everybody around here tried to be high and mighty."

Growing impatient, the doctor threw most of the remaining letters into an empty box. One of them, however, seemed to be in an old man's hand, and he picked it up again. It was from the fellow in Detroit who had bought the place on tax sale:

"Dear Mrs. Clatry,
"I received your kind letter and was glad to hear from you. I am sending you the $30 toward the new cellar doors and the work on the barn and the rest you pay yourself. I aint charging you no rent until spring till I see what I am going to do. Let me know if you received the money right away. You say the plum trees are in blossom. Glad to hear you like them, it is a very quiet place and I think that sycamore is a very nice tree. There was two trees but when the other shed burnt down that one other tree burnt too. I guess when the Lord comes he will come like a thief in the night,

nobody knows when that will be but it begins to look it won't be so long for his coming. I am getting tired of working in factories and when your beginning to get up in years you cant take it like a young person. It sure gets on your nerves. Too bad your husband did not try the pump before he went for the well man. I hope your husband is working steady and I wish you the best of luck. Let me know right away if you received the money. I must ring off with my best regards to both of you.
"Yours very truly,
William Rogerson"

Apparently this communication had never been acknowledged by the Clatrys. It was followed by three more notes, of increasing anxiety, from old Rogerson, asking if the money had arrived. Nothing had been done, the doctor reflected, about the old cellar door and the sagging barn.

Only three or four more letters remained in the doctor's hand. He swore softly in surprise at the next, from a Clifford Billings of Eugenia, Michigan. It was in ink; the capital letters had been encircled in red, as if Mrs. Clatry had sat musing over it; it was undated:

"Mrs. Ella Clatry,
"Dear Club member, I saw your ad. in the Joined Hands Club and thought I would like to know you. I am looking for a true and good woman, either not married or a widow. I have one little girl eight next month and she needs a good mother and I too need a nice Cook and mate. I am very active and healthy and therefore should have a nice Wife to love. My earnest Prayer is to find a nice true woman to love.
"I am a Farmer and Berry grower, have a place that can be made to a nice Home with the help of a good woman.
"So if you are still looking for a nice fellow that is kind

and true I would be glad to hear from you in the near future and would appreciate a Picture."

* * *

"Well, I guess we've got everything we want, Doctor," called out Frank, scrambling down the stairs with the chevrons and the garrison cap. Harry had salvaged a shaving mug and a jackknife with one blade snapped. The doctor looked again at the farmer's letter, frowned, and followed the boys through the house and out at the back door, still carrying a couple of soiled letters. Mrs. Bass having packed sandwiches for the three of them, they sat on the sparse grass in the shade of the sycamore to have their lunch.

Biting an apple, the doctor glanced at one of the remaining pieces of paper—a dun from a jewelry shop.

"Dear Madam: We have on our books an account by the name of Gerald Clatry. It is in the amount of $47.53, for a gold wedding ring with small diamond, purchased June 5, 1946. We understand Mr. Clatry is deceased. Can you advise as to what is being done by his estate on matters such as this?"

Dead? The doctor pulled the last letter from its envelope. A Mrs. Alonzo Clatry had sent it:

"Ella,
"I am writing to ask if you would give your consent to have Jerry's body taken up and laid to rest in the cemetery where nearly all our folks are buried. My father took up land from the government when Ohio was being settled and the farm has always been in our family. If you leave the place where you are now, there would be no one to put flowers on his grave. He never was a boy to hang around home, so

when he came back from the war and was married I was so happy thinking he would settle down and I could see him often.

"While I was looking through some boxes I run across a letter he wrote in a foxhole and I set down and cried thinking how things had turned out; he was so young to die, and to think he believed I never wanted to see him again.

"I hope you will forgive little Helen for talking the way she did, about your marrying Jerry. Children take things so hard.

"Sincerely,
"Alice Clatry
"(Mrs. Alonzo Clatry)"

The doctor put down his apple. "Did Mr. Clatry die right here?"

"Yes," said Harry, finishing his sandwich, "but Mrs. Clatry stayed on for a month. She tried to go to some of the neighbors, but nobody wanted to take five kids, and besides she wasn't well liked. Some people were scared of her. After Mr. Clatry went, the Whittakers could hear her walloping the kids half a mile away. She was on edge. Toward the end of the month, she told people she was going to stay the summer and then go north and get married again. But one night the Whittakers heard her screeching, and Pat went over, and she squealed that somebody had been peeking in the windows and trying the doors. It's a lonesome house. Pat says she looked like something loose from the crazy house. Next morning she walked into town with the kids, just carrying a suitcase, and they all took the bus, and nobody's heard from them since."

"Mr. Clatry died *right* here," declared Frank, reminiscently. He pointed to the nearest strong limb of the sycamore. "There was where he hung himself."

"Where he was hanging when the Whittakers found him, that is," added Harry, in the tone of one entrusted with family gossip. "There were lumps and bruises all over him, but probably Mrs. Clatry left marks on him most days, anyway. She'd gone after groceries when the Whittakers came along the road and saw Mr. Clatry hanging. People didn't like it, but Mr. Clatry hadn't any relations around here, and he was buried without much more said."

"Look!" demanded Frank, putting on the garrison cap and sucking in his cheeks. "Look, I'm Mr. Clatry!"

A breeze, rustling the sycamore, picked a dozen grains of sand from beside the doctor's feet and deposited them on his shoes. Grasshoppers leaped in the sun; two crows alighted on a stump fence across the sand road; as the wind touched it, the barn door creaked heavily. Had it not been for the boys beside him, the doctor thought he would have run straight across the barren, despite the sand, until he gained cover in the cedar swamp.

EX TENEBRIS

🔔

> Then shall it be too late to knock when the door shall be shut; and too late to cry for mercy when it is the time of justice. O terrible voice of the most just judgment which shall be pronounced upon them, when shall it be said unto them, Go ye cursed into the fire everlasting, which is prepared for the devil and his angels.
> —A Commination, or Denouncing of God's Anger and Judgments against Sinners

Only one roof at Low Wentford is sound today. On either side of the lane, a row of stone cottages stands empty. Twenty years ago there were three times as many; but now the rest are rubble. A gutted shell of Victorian masonry is the ruin of the schoolhouse. Close by the brook, the church of All Saints stares drearily into its desolate graveyard; a good fifteenth-century building, All Saints, but the glass smashed in its windows and the slates slipping one after another from the roof. It has been deconsecrated all this century. Beside it, the vicarage—after the soldiers quartered there had finished with it—was demolished for the sake of what its woodwork and fittings would bring.

In the last sound cottage lives Mrs. Oliver, an ancient little woman with a nose that very nearly meets her chin.

She wears a countrywoman's cloak of the old pattern, and weeds her garden, and sometimes walks as far as the high-arched bridge which, built long before the cottages, has survived them. Mrs. Oliver has no neighbors nearer than the Oghams of Wentford House, a mile down a bedraggled avenue of limes and beeches twisting through the neglected park to the stables of that Queen Anne mansion.

Nearly three years ago, Sir Gerald Ogham sold the cottage to Mrs. Oliver, who had come back from Madras to the village where she was born. In all the parish, no one remained who remembered Mrs. Oliver. She had gone out to India with her husband, the Major; no one knew how long ago that had been—not even Mrs. Oliver, perhaps—with any precision, for she had known Sir Gerald's father, but had grown vague about decades and such trifles. Sir Gerald himself, though he was past sixty, could recollect of her only that her name had been an old one in the village.

Village? Like the money of the Oghams, it had faded quite away: the Ogham fortunes and Low Wentford now were close to extinction. The wealth of the Oghams was gone to the wars and the Exchequer; the last of the villagers had been drained away to the mills at Gorst, when tractors had supplanted horses upon the farms which Sir Gerald had sold to a potato syndicate. Behind the shutters of the sixty rooms of Wentford House, a solitary daily woman did what she could to supply the place of twenty servants. Lady Ogham and the gardener and the gardener's boy grew flowers and vegetables in the walled garden, to be sold in Gorst; Sir Gerald, with a feckless bailiff and a half-dozen laborers, struggled to wrest a few hundred pounds' income from the home farm and the few fields he had left besides.

The family name still meaning something roundabout, Sir Gerald sat in the county council, where he sided with a forlorn minority overborne by the councillors from sprawling Gorst.

Sir Gerald had tried to sell the other habitable cottages in Low Wentford; but the planning officer, backed by the sanitary officer, had put obstacles in the way. And it was only because they had been unable at the time to provide a council-flat for old Mrs. Oliver that they had permitted her to repair the cottage near the church. The windows were too small, the sanitary officer and the planning officer had said; but Mrs. Oliver had murmured that in Madras she had seen enough of the sun to last her all her days. The ceilings were lower than regulations specified; but Mrs. Oliver had replied that the coal ration would go the further for that. It must be damp, the sanitary officer felt sure; but he was unable to prove it. There were no communal amenities, said the planning officer; but Mrs. Oliver, deaf as well as dim of sight, told him she disliked Communists. The authorities yielding, Mrs. Oliver had moved in with her Indian keepsakes and her few sticks of furniture, proceeding to train rosebushes against the old walls and to spade her own little garden; for, despite her great age, she was not feeble of body or of will.

Mr. S. G. W. Barner, Planning Officer, had a will of his own, nevertheless, and he had made up his mind that not one stone was to be left upon another at Low Wentford. With satisfaction he had seen the last of the farm-laborers of that hamlet transferred to the new council houses at Gorst, where there was no lack of communal facilities, including six cinemas. Thus were they integrated with the progressive aspirations of planned industrial society, he told the county council. Privately, he was convinced that the agricultural laborer ought to be liquidated altogether. And why not? Advanced planning, within a few years, surely would liberate progressive societies from dependence upon old-fashioned farming. He disliked the whole notion of agriculture, with its rude earthiness, its reactionary views of life and labor, its subservience to tradition. The agricultural classes would be absorbed into the centers of population, or otherwise disposed of; the land thus placed at public command would be converted into garden cities, or state holiday-camps, or proving grounds for industrial and military experiment.

With a positive passion of social indignation then, S. G. W. Barner—a thick-chested, hairy man, forever carrying a dispatch case, stooping and heavy of tread, rather like a large, earnest ape (as Sir Gerald had observed to Lady Ogham, after an unpleasant encounter at a county council meeting)—objected against Mrs. Oliver's tenancy of the little red-tiled cottage. His consolation had been that she had not long to live, being wrinkled and gnarled amazingly. To his chagrin, however, she seemed to thrive in the loneliness of Low Wentford, her cheeks growing rosier, her step more sure. She must be got out of that cottage by compulsory purchase, if nothing else would serve. On Mr. Barner's maps of the Rural District of Low Wentford as it would be in the future, there remained no vexatious dots to represent cottages by the old bridge; nor was there any little cross to represent the derelict church. (No church had yet been erected in the newest housing scheme at Gorst: Cultural Amenities must yield pride of place to material requirements, Barner had declared.)

Yes, that wreck of a church must come down, with what remained of Low Wentford. Ruins are reminiscent of the past; and the Past is a dead hand impeding progressive planning. Besides, Low Wentford had been a hamlet immediately dependent upon Wentford House and its baronets, and therefore ought to be effaced as an obsolete fragment of a repudiated social order. It was disconcerting that even a doddering old creature like the obdurate Mrs. Oliver should prefer living in this unhealthy rurality; and now a council-flat could be made available to her. She would be served a compulsory purchase order before long, if the Planning Officer had his way—which he was accustomed to have—and would be moved to Gorst where she belonged. The surviving cottages might be condemned to demolition as a public nuisance, Sir Gerald's obscurantism notwithstanding. What should be done with the cleared site of Low Wentford? Why, it might be utilized as a dump for earth excavated in the Gorst housing schemes. That obsolete bridge, incidentally, ought to be replaced by a level concrete one.

"Let a decent old woman keep her roses," Sir Gerald had said to the Planning Officer when last they met in Gorst. "Why do you whirl her off to your jerry-built desolation of concrete roadways that you've designed, so far as I can see, to make it difficult for people to get about on foot? Why do you have to make her live under the glare of mercury vapor lamps and listen to other people's wireless sets when she wants quiet? Sometimes I think a devil's got inside you, Barner."

With dignity, S. G. W. Barner felt, he had replied to this tirade. "I am very much afraid, Sir Gerald, that you don't understand the wants of common human beings. Elderly members of the community need to be kept under the supervision of social workers and local authorities, for their own welfare; indeed, I trust the time is not far distant when residence in eventide homes will be compulsory upon all aged persons, regardless of fancied social distinctions. Mrs. Oliver requires relief from her self-imposed isolation."

"You're no better than a walking bluebook, Barner," Sir Gerald Ogham had answered—red as a beet, the Planning Officer recollected with relish—and had stamped away. Opposition from such a quarter was sufficient evidence of the need for taking Mrs. Oliver and Low Wentford in hand so soon as the Council would be wheeled into action. He must find time to draw up a persuasive report on the redundancy of Low Wentford.

* * *

In truth, Low Wentford *was* a lonely place, as Mrs. Oliver confessed to herself, though she knew it never would do to tell Mr. Barner so. Some things she seemed to forget, nowadays, but she knew whom she could trust and whom she could not. Lady Ogham came to visit her occasionally, bringing a present of fruit or flowers; otherwise, Mrs. Oliver was quite alone. Despite being deaf and nearsighted and English, she had enjoyed more company in Madras. How long was it since the Major had gone? She had little notion. Sometimes children, straggling down from the potato-syndicate farm, ran from her in fright, here in the village where she had been born; children never dreaded her in Madras.

But she wanted no more visits from the Planning Officer. She knew what he was about. He had come last week—or was it last month?—and she had made him shout properly, saying she was sorry to be deaf, though really she had understood him well enough when he spoke in a lower key. She had shaken her head again and again and again. She had bought this cottage, and it was hers, and she loved her roses, and she did not want to be cared for. He had turned from her quite disagreeable. It was something about maps. And communal amenities. He would not stay for tea, although she had told him that she still baked her own bread. Mr. Barner was a cheerless man, and he frightened her. Had he said something about an old witch when he banged the door after him?

Certainly he had said he was out of patience. Almost nothing in India had frightened her: the riots would not have made her come home; it was only that she had longed to see the country round Low Wentford, even though all the old neighbors were gone. But she was afraid of Mr. Barner, because he seemed more unchristian than any Indian, worshipping his maps. And he might do something about her cottage. Sir Gerald, if she had understood him properly, had said as much. She would not go to Gorst; it was not a nice place, not nice at all, even when she was young. And naughty children in such places pointed at her nose, and at her stick. If only there were a neighbor or two . . . Sir Gerald and Lady Ogham were busy people; and, too, she needed someone less grand. Why was it that the vicar never came to call? Though she had been reared a Methodist, she could recollect the plump old vicar of All Saints, Low Wentford. Was it he who had married her to the Major? She thought so. But she supposed that he, like the Major, was gone. Perhaps the vicar could have helped her against Mr. S. G. W. Barner. Really, she had come to hate Mr. Barner. She had been reasonably good most of her life, and so felt entitled to hate a man or two, at her age. Parsons knew how to manage such people. Did the vicar know she was living in Low Wentford again? Had anyone told him?

He must have more than one parish, surely, and have been too busy to call upon her as yet. For the church was locked always. She had tried the door a number of times, especially on Sundays, but it never yielded. She supposed the vicar must come late Sunday evening, after she had gone to bed; indeed, she thought—though she could not be sure— that she had seen lights, like little candles, moving within the church, once or twice when she had risen in the middle of the night to shut a window against the rain. Doubtless he would call eventually, this poor harried vicar, and she would give him tea and her own scones. Meanwhile, she had her cat to talk with; and a fine great cat he was, named Bentinck, and she could tell Bentinck of the iniquities of Mr. Barner. The milkman came in the morning, and the grocer's van in the afternoon—that was company. But the vanmen were ever so shy: you would have thought them afraid of her. Should she fall ill, now, the vicar would be duty bound to call on her. Her health invariably was good, however—more's the pity—better than ever it had been in Madras. Lady Ogham told her, laughing a little, that she was so hale and rosy she seemed more than human. "My flowers and my oven keep me brisk, Lady Ogham," she had said, stroking Bentinck.

Though it had been disused for years before she came, the cottage oven was a good one. She baked little sweet cakes of all shapes and dimensions. Being very ill-tempered the day after Mr. Barner had visited her, she had made of dough one cake that looked quite like the Planning Officer, and deliberately left it too long in the oven so that it burnt black, and Bentinck would not touch it even when it was soaked in milk. But that had been spiteful. She wished she did not have to think about Mr. Barner. Perhaps if she went out of the cottage more often, he would not come creeping into her mind. She ought to cross to the churchyard every evening, to forget the poor menaced cottage for a while; and there she might look at the tombstones, if she should take a little broom with her to brush the leaves away. She knew many of the folk that lay by the church, and it would be pleasant to sit among them in the sunset.

When had she decided this? Had it been last autumn? Or had it been only a fortnight ago? Nowadays she came daily, before sunset, to the churchyard and swept the gravestones. It being March, often rain came while she was there; then she sat in the south porch of the church, wrapped in her cloak and hood, and took no harm. Always the church door was locked, but that did not much matter, for everyone whose name she could remember was buried to the south of the church, not inside. She brushed with her little broom, and found Aunt Polly and Grandfather Thomas, and Ann with whom she had played in the schoolyard, and even the plump old vicar, who, she recalled now, had been the Reverend Henry Williams. But they were not altogether satisfactory as neighbors, for of course she could see them only in memory, and they could not answer. They did not succeed in keeping Mr. S. G. W. Barner from creeping in the back of her mind. He was detestable.

Except for the fallen limbs of old rowans and the hig[h] damp grass, the south side of the churchyard was a cheerf[ul] place, far better than the north side. The graves were fe[w] on that latter cold and windy slope, and the weeds we[re] thicker, and everything seemed squalid. She would ha[ve] liked to tell the vicar so. A small porch clung to that si[de] of the church, too, but she dared not sit there, for even s[he] could perceive that the heavy porch roof threatened collapse. Probably Sir Gerald Ogham was not able to mai[n]tain All Saints as his father had done. A little low archway, she supposed it was the Normans' work—led from the por[ch] into the tower. Sometimes it seemed to her that the door [in] the archway was ajar; but she could not make certain, f[or] when she approached once, a slate fell right at her feet, a[nd] she feared she might bring the whole porch down upon h[er] head. If this was the way the vicar entered the church, [he] must be rather a heedless man. She could not remember t[he] door ever having been opened when she was a girl.

No, she did not like the north side. Having swept all t[he] gravestones to the south, however, she felt that really s[he] ought to treat the folk on the north equally well. One ev[e]ning, then, she found herself brushing the thick wet leav[es] from a slab close by the north porch. Was there a nam[e] upon it? She put on her spectacles and, leaning on her stic[k,] bent as close as she could. Then a shadow fell across the sla[b.]

Mrs. Oliver turned sharp round, thinking that perha[ps] Mr. Barner had come again. But it was someone else: [a] parson, a tall man with a long, long face, hatched lines cros[s]ing on forehead and cheeks. She could see him more plain[ly] than she could see most people. He must have come from the little doorway under the tower. He was nothing like the old vicar, Mr. Williams. This would be his successor, and it was good that he had come. Drops of moisture ran from his long black hair down the furrows in his sad face, so he must have walked a great way in the rain.

"I am Mrs. Oliver," she said. Why did she have trouble getting the words out?

Though clear, his voice was harsh and grating; he did not seem to be speaking loudly, unlike everybody else, who shouted at her. "I am Abner Hargreaves," he said, "your vicar."

* * *

"Something curious happened today," Sir Gerald Ogham remarked to his wife, at dinner. He stared at a place on the high ceiling where the faded Chinese paper was peeling, and paused, as if he regretted having spoken.

"Well?" said Lady Ogham. "You know, this room is falling to bits. What was strange?"

"Mrs. Oliver was odd," Sir Gerald told her. "You'd best say nothing of this to anyone, Alice: if Barner knew, it might improve his case."

"Odd? I always have thought her a sensible old dear, aside from her way of talking to that monstrous cat as though he were a viceroy."

"Perhaps it was only some person passing through the village on his way to Gorst," Sir Gerald went on. "But she said the vicar came to call, yesterday evening, and took tea with her."

"Vicar? Whom could she have meant, Gerald? Mr. Harris, of Holy Trinity, in Gorst?"

"Harris has nothing to do with this parish; besides, he scarcely bothers to call anywhere in Gorst. He knows he has emoluments to receive, but forgets he has duties to perform. He never would have been poking about a deconsecrated church. And you know what a frail reed Harris is, while this fellow seems to have been a strapping parson of the old breed. Mrs. Oliver was quite overawed by him; I had thought nothing could make such a distinct impression on her—though she did forget his name while she was talking with me. I wish I had seen him. It never would do for word to get about that Mrs. Oliver talks with shadows: in no time, Barner would have her off to some insufferable eventide home. Yet I do believe—if I understood her—that she fancies the church still is in use."

"Oh, no, Gerald, really she can't! It must have been shut when she was a girl here."

"No, All Saints has not been derelict that long. I was a half-grown boy before they locked it. Even then, it was in a bad way; almost no one but our family used to attend. There were few parishioners left about Low Wentford, and the vicar offended most of those few. He was remarkably harsh, fond of nothing but the cursing psalms and Jeremiah. I recollect a commination, on Ash Wednesday—which, by the way, is nearly upon us again, Alice—that gave me nightmares. Then the scandal put an end to things, and they took the furniture and the bells away to Gorst. One of these days the whole roof will fall through."

"You never told me of a scandal."

"A nasty story, Alice. The village schoolmaster was the village atheist—Rally was his name, or Reddy. The vicar loathed this schoolmaster, who, he said, was corrupting the parish. It was against Reddy the vicar preached that commination I remember. How he cursed him! When Reddy heard what had been said, he came round to face the vicar out. Both of them had beastly tempers.

"During the first week of Lent, Reddy was found in the brook by the bridge, his neck broken. Like most convinced atheists, he drank, however, and he might have fallen from the bridge to the stones, in the night."

"Do you mean the poor vicar was slandered merely on that coincidence?"

"No. Of itself, Reddy's death might have been passed over. Even the vicar's death might have been passed over; for he was found drowned in our quarry six months later. He might have been bathing. It was a clause in his will that caused the talk—that, and his sermons and the look on his face for months before. He left instructions that he should be buried on the north side of the church, 'with other murderers and perjurers and suicides, that burn forever.' The vicar was eloquent, as if inspired by angels; but what sort of angels, people wondered. How he talked of sinners in the hands of an angry God! Whatever he was, he thundered like the agent of Omnipotence. Yet Satan, for that matter . . . I believe his name was Harbound, or Harcourt, or Harbottle; but it doesn't signify any longer, except conceivably to the vicar himself, poor damned soul."

* * *

Nearly every evening, now, Mr. Hargreaves came to call and Mrs. Oliver was comforted. Though he was in no sense a cheerful being, she was convinced that he possessed immense powers of sympathy. He sat moodily in his corner away from the fire, always dripping, somehow, even when Mrs. Oliver had thought the evening fair; and Mrs. Oliver told him her tribulations. He would eat nothing, yet he drank her tea with a prodigious thirst; and he seemed to need it, for his voice was fearfully dry and harsh; and to judge by his eyes, he suffered from malaria. She wished that she might hear him preach: he held a command of language she never before had encountered in a parson. But when she asked him about the hours of service, he did not seem to hear her. Bentinck, temperamental, wailed whenever Mr. Hargreaves entered, fleeing to the top of the cupboard, whence he spat at the vicar; but the Reverend Abner Hargreaves took no notice of the cat. Now and again he spoke at length, with wonderful passion, as clearly as he had spoken when first they met in the churchyard; and he seemed to anticipate her every thought. Mr. Barner, she told the vicar, was a wicked man.

"Cursed is he that perverteth the judgment of the stranger, the fatherless and widow," said Mr. Hargreaves.

"I wish you would speak to him," said Mrs. Oliver.

"All thine enemies shall feel thy hand; thy right hand shall find them out that hate thee," continued Mr. Hargreaves, almost chanting. "Thou shalt make them like a fiery oven in time of thy wrath; the Lord shall destroy them in his displeasure, and the fire shall consume them."

"I don't wish him any harm," said Mrs. Oliver, "but he *is* wicked."

At that, Mr. Hargreaves rose abruptly, and went out of the cottage into the night. Mrs. Oliver hoped that she had not somehow offended him. But at all times he came and went unceremoniously. No doubt Mr. Hargreaves was zealous; yet he was not quite a cheering vicar.

* * *

Mr. S. G. W. Barner sat in his study, amusing himself by drawing up plans for a model collective agricultural unit adapted to British agronomy—something he did not intend to show to the county council, nevertheless, or at least not to a council of its present complexion—when a bell rang, and rang again, faintly.

"Susan, *will* you answer that?" he called to his wife, in annoyance.

"Answer what, dear?" his wife inquired, from the corridor.

"The doorbell, of course," Barner told her, fidgeting with his ruler.

She was back in a moment. "No one . . ." Then he heard the faint bell again.

"The telephone, Susan," said Barner. "Must I manage every trifling detail in this household?" She bit her lip and hurried out.

"No one telephoned either," she called, in a moment. "And I never heard it ring, dear."

Flinging down his ruler, Barner strode into the hall, and snatched the receiver from her. "Nonsense! Of course it rang!" And someone was speaking, as he had expected. Barner nodded contemptuously to his wife, who shrank into the kitchen.

The voice was deep, afflicted with a parched hoarseness. For some seconds, Barner thought he had the receiver wrong end to, or that something was amiss with the instrument; but then the voice sounded more distinctly.

". . . without delay," it was saying. "I have spoken with Mrs. Oliver. The thing must be done with."

Barner gathered that the agent, whoever he was, desired a meeting. "Where?" asked Barner. This might be an opportunity to clear away the Low Wentford annoyance. "When?"

"At All Saints," said the voice, with something like a gasp, and then paused, almost as if the idea of Time (Barner wondered why this foolish fancy passed through his brain) were alien to the speaker. "We meet," said the parched voice, "at once."

"In the dark?" protested Barner. "You've called far too late. Tuesday, possibly."

"This night, at All Saints, Low Wentford." The voice, imperious, startled Barner.

"Whoever are you?" he asked.

"Hargreaves, the vicar. I am waiting." Then there was silence. Barner put down the telephone after an attempt to remonstrate to the void.

Well, the hour would do well enough, after all; but he would be short with this cantankerous vicar. Vicar of what? Barner knew no Hargreaves. Some relative, conceivably, of Mrs. Oliver. He was tempted to let the silly parson, with his bad manners, wait all night in the churchyard. Then, though, he might lose his chance to finish with Low Wentford. Telling his wife that he would return in an hour or two, Barner got into his automobile and drove out of the villadom that hems in Gorst toward Low Wentford.

* * *

As Barner switched off his ignition, it occurred to him that the churchyard of All Saints was a cheerless place to meet this fellow. The mist from the brook drifted upwards toward the church. Could they not have talked in that old woman's confounded cottage? It was wet here, and hard to tell haar from stone. With proper employment of scientific methodology, one day society would plan its weather, perhaps eliminating altogether the seasons. But for the stupidity of entrenched interests, the thing would have been accomplished already. Superstition! Today, for instance, was some irrational relic of superstitious rubbish—Ash Wednesday, that was it. Barner walked through the tangled grass toward the south porch. He saw no one. Would this vicar have a key to let them in, or must they parley in the drizzle?

No one stood in this porch. Barner thought he caught a glimmer of light within the church; but this door was bolted. He blundered round to the north side. As he approached the small porch by the tower, someone stalked out to meet him.

The vicar was a man of great stature; it was too dark for Barner to perceive much more of him, though he recognized at once the parched and rasping voice. "I ask you, sir, for charity," said this vicar, out of the fog.

"If you mean that old woman down the lane, Mr. Hargreaves," Barner interrupted, "the most charitable thing we can do is to re-house her where amenities and social intercourse are available." Though the vicar had come up close to him, Barner could not see his face well enough, through the mist, to make out his cast of countenance. It would be the face of a sentimental fool, Barner knew. They stood in the lee of the north porch, the grass up to their knees, some slippery slab underfoot; and a wind had risen, damply cutting.

"Who are you, sir," the vicar went on—his throat seemingly dry as an oven—"and what am I, to meddle with an old woman's longing? She called me from a great way to do her this service; and I must have your charity, or else you must seek mine; and now I have none to give. 'Cursed is he that perverteth the judgment of the stranger, the fatherless and widow.' Do you know the verse which stands next to that, man? It is this: 'Cursed is he that smiteth his neighbor secretly.' In the universe are vicars of more sorts than one, but I am bound by special ordinances; and therefore I do entreat you, sir, to call it to mind that this woman's house is as the breath of life to her. The breath of life, man. Think what that means!"

Well, reflected Barner, here's the old-world Bible-thumper with a vengeance. "Individual preferences often must be subordinated to communal efficiency," was what he said.

"I speak not simply of whim and inclination," the vicar caught him up, "but of the memories of childhood and girlhood, the pieties that cling to our hearth, however desolated."

"That's rot you're talking, you know," Barner objected, exasperated. Did the vicar step closer to him? Barner shifted backward through the grass, so that he stood just within the porch. "Candidly, I consider parsons just so many impediments to social unity. Leave sociology to trained minds, Mr. Hargreaves. I see you have not the faintest conception of the essentials of planning. I have an Act of Parliament at my back. Who authorized you to meddle with official programmes? Perhaps some people desire your services: old Mrs. Oliver, for instance, possibly extracts some solace from your Bible stories. I do not."

The vicar laughed. Barner never had heard a laugh like it —a sound nearer the braying of a mule than anything from a man's throat. It was indescribably dismal. "Blind, blind," the vicar declared. "His fan is in his hand, and he will purge his floor, and gather his wheat into the barn, but he will burn the chaff with unquenchable fire. For the sake of a void upon a map, man, would you cast away your hope of salvation?"

"Salvation?" asked Barner, with a shrug. "Salvation? I came to you for a practical settlement, not a sermon. I want that woman out of her cottage."

"I have said all that it was required I should say," the vicar answered, "and have done all that it was required I should do." His voice was exhortatory no longer; now a quality of devouring eagerness was in it. He took another step toward Barner, who at last saw his face distinctly.

A sentimental parson? Not this man. The jaw, long and rock-like; the cheeks, seamed and hollow; the pallid, pallid skin; the high-bridged nose, with distended nostrils; the red and staring eyes, with the look of a beast in torment—these were thrust close up to Barner's face in the gloom of the porch. Enormous beads of water or sweat ran down the vicar's cheeks.

"But I do ask you, this last time," said the vicar, "for charity."

Or did he say it? His lips had not moved. And abruptly it came to Barner that the vicar's lips had not stirred before; that rigid face was a mask; and the words Barner had thought he heard had sounded only in his own brain, not in his ears. Even in the telephone . . . Barner clutched a stone bench-end within the porch. What tricks the dark and the mist played! Of course the vicar's lips must have moved; no one would play ventriloquist in this place. "No," insisted Barner, scowling, his assurance partially recovered, "I never grant exceptions to any scheduled scheme." How loathsome that parson's features were! "I say, Vicar, if you must talk of this longer, sha'n't we shift out of this wind and wet into the church?" For Barner wanted mightily to put some interval between himself and that waxy face.

"Safe in the church? You and I? Never!" cried the parson, in a voice at once exultant and agonized. He smiled frightfully. "For now is the axe put to the root of the trees, so that every tree that bringeth forth not good fruit, is hewn down and cast into the fire." Then he took Barner by the throat.

* * *

For more than a week, the curious death of S. G. W. Barner was a subject of conversation even beyond Gorst; the *Review of Collective Planning* observed that in Barner, pragmatic social reconstruction had lost one of its more promising younger advocates. Apparently Barner had been making a brief inspection of the derelict church of All Saints, which he intended to persuade the ecclesiastical authorities to demolish, when the roof of the north porch, weakened by incompetent restorers near the end of the eighteenth century and further imperilled by neglect, fell upon him. His body was not discovered until the following afternoon.

Two or three of Barner's acquaintances remarked that he would have been vexed by a cultural lag connected with his cremation. The suffragan bishop of Wandersley, within whose cure Gorst lies, recently had spoken with vigor against the "barbarous practice" of scattering the ashes, after cremation, at random over unconsecrated ground; while the Reverend John Harris, vicar of Holy Trinity, Old Gorst, protested against the strewing of ashes within his churchyard, as offensive to the sensibilities of his parishioners and his wife. The undertaker and Mrs. Barner, therefore, were in some perplexity, until Mr. Harris suggested that the churchyard of Low Wentford might be suitable, there being no clergyman in residence, and the only person who might possibly object being Sir Gerald Ogham. Consulted, Sir Gerald said that, the Ogham tombs lying to the south of All Saints, these ashes ought to be strewn on the north side of the churchyard. This was done; and Sir Gerald, though not present on the occasion, told the county sanitary officer that he thought no ceremony could have been more fitting.

The county council has relinquished the scheme for clearing the site of Low Wentford; indeed, there appears to be some possibility that six or seven of the cottages near the bridge may be restored, with the aid of grants from local authorities, as part of a plan of deconcentration recommended by the new planning officer. Mrs. Oliver's cottage, in any event, seems secure. She weeds her garden, and bakes her scones, and often sweeps the gravestones clean; thus she continues surprisingly vigorous for a woman of her years. Though the vicar no longer calls, as she told Lady Ogham one day, instead she has a new confidant—a Mr. Reddy, highly opinionated, given to denying the existence of Heaven, and suffering dreadfully from some old injury to his neck.

THE SURLY SULLEN BELL

🔔

Having stared at the river for half an hour, Loring walked back across the great steel bridge and turned to the left. A little past eight he would have to be knocking at the Schumachers'.

In St. Louis they have pounded the Old Town into dust. All along the Mississippi, where the little city of the French and their American successors used to lie, now is a brick-strewn desolation—no building standing but the stiff old cathedral, grudgingly spared in the fiat which destined this belt of land for a memorial park. To the modern politician and planner, men are the flies of a summer, oblivious of their past, reckless of their future. Governmental contracts and newspaper publicity are concrete; the Old Town had been only a shabby slum to the politicians and planners of St. Louis, men not given to long views or to theory.

So Frank Loring thought as he strolled down one of those forlorn streets of condemned houses that cling to a brief reprieve on the edge of the bulldozed wilderness that once was an historic community. Loring was not progressive. Candidly, Loring told himself, he was a reactionary. Ecclesiastes was Bible enough for him. Though not yet forty, he had beheld nearly all things under the sun, he thought; and yesterday's sun had been warmer than today's. St. Louis being a progressive town, in which the air stank from the breweries and the government stank from other fermentation, Loring stopped there only when God and Mammon called him.

As traveller for a publishing firm, he could not keep away altogether from dingy St. Louis, with its vast stupid "civic center" and its decaying heart; but until this evening he had held the Gomorrah of a city at arm's length, sticking chiefly to his hotel room in the grandiose late-Victorian railway station. Tonight, though, the past had claimed him.

For Professor Schumacher had found Loring. Professor Schumacher was Godfrey Schumacher, the husband of Mrs. Nancy Schumacher; and Nancy had been Nancy Birrell; and all this past decade Loring had not seen her, praise be. She was very lovable; and being no Stoic Frank Loring had chosen not to look upon her since she married. Ten years, all the same—some healing power, surely, in such a quarantine by time. Well, he would see her tonight beside her husband and talk of little things, and then plod back into apathy.

He had been sitting at a soda fountain with an instructor in literature when there came up Godfrey Schumacher, professor of Spanish, with whom he hadn't spoken for ten years either; and Schumacher had shaken his hand and smiled his old lordly smile and asked him to come round for an evening with Nancy and himself. Loring must have shown his surprise. "Nancy hoped I'd be able to persuade you," Schumacher said. "She speaks of you often." And Schumacher had put a large, patronizing hand on Loring's shoulder. "They told me in the dean's office you were expected in town this week, Frank."

Nancy hoped? Why? That was what Loring wanted to ask; but instead he had smiled and agreed and lamented the day's heat, and complimented Schumacher on the grey suit he wore. Schumacher cut nearly as handsome a figure as he had a decade gone, and much of his past-president-of-fraternity air had survived, too. Mingled with it was a hint of something newer and perhaps deeper—a kind of frowning dignity, even an intensity. Again Loring was a trifle surprised, Schumacher not having been the sort of man one expects to ripen with the years. And somehow Loring relished these recent developments of Schumacher's nature no more than he had liked the old Schumacher.

Schumacher wasn't the man he'd spend an evening with if he hadn't been cornered and almost bluffed into it. As for Nancy . . . What could she and Loring have to say now that wouldn't hurt? Every smile must be a reflection of past folly, every civility a humiliation. And natty, broad-shouldered, merry-dog Schumacher there between them, now and to the end of time. Well, what *did* Nancy mean to say to him? For she must have been at the back of Schumacher's invitation. They'd hardly known each other, Schumacher and he, back in those days before the Great Fact; and when they had met—a half-dozen times perhaps—there'd been no love lost. Twice a year, for five years now, Loring had been coming round to St. Louis, but Schumacher never once had sought him out.

Ah, that was Nancy's doing, that impulsive little girl's doing. Little girl? She must be thirty-five, nearly. Yet to his mind she was the wind-blown romp beside the lake in the pine woods, calling out "Frank! Frank! Do I look like Carmen?" And so she would stay for him always.

A scent brought back Loring from the lake in the woods, a dozen years lost, to the pavements of St. Louis and the present. To be detected through the air of downtown St. Louis, this scent must be a stench. Such it was, and it came from the doorways of the condemned houses past which Loring was sauntering. Their windows broken, their doors gone, their steps rotted, their chimneys fallen away, still these houses were inhabited in a sparse and furtive way. To this slum of slums crawled down the most pitiful and foul sweepings of the white populace of a great city: old men with no legs who played harmonicas outside the picture-houses at night; women wrecked by liquor; grown imbeciles subsisting on restaurant garbage; the torpid, the loathsome, the soddenly vicious. They lit fires on sheet-iron scrap in the bare rooms, and slept wrapped in newspapers or filthy old coats; they got water the devil knew where—from the river, perhaps. The stench of them and their litter, the remnants of their greasy suppers and their carpet of dust, swept sourly into the street.

Without plumbing, without heating, without lighting, they lived on in these wrecks of houses, while the plaster flaked away with damp and the rats gnawed the timbers. For condemned houses that were the last stand of the Old Town had this surpassing advantage: no one collected rent. Their site was the state's, their walls were the wreckers', and the police of St. Louis left the squatters in possession as creatures too unclean and too futile for touching.

These old houses were flush with the street, and alleys, courts, dead-end lanes opened from the sidewalk into the back recesses of the few doomed blocks—bad warrens to enter if you looked a bit under the weather and ripe for rolling. Loring quickened his pace, it being nearly dark now and the Schumachers' address five or six blocks further. He stepped over the legs of a burly man who slouched immobile upon the steps of a tenement; and he noticed that though the fellow wore no shirt this summer evening, a thick woollen undershirt covered him from neck to wrists, and that the man's head, nearly bald, had a great nasty protuberance, almost conical, on one side. Pleasant neighbors for the Schumachers, these squatters of the condemned streets.

A little further along he met an old, or at least haggard, man and woman lurching toward him, bleary and raucous. As they scurried past, the woman threw up a grimy hand like a witch's right in his face, screeching out, "Ah there, lover!" And now Loring had found the house number Schumacher had given him: a square, bracketed house, decently kept, with a brick wall round it—the beginning of that mid-Victorian girdle which marched with the fringe of the older town.

In his diffident way, Loring went slowly up the walk, raised his hand to knock, and then lowered it. Who would answer? Would Nancy be face to face with him the second the door opened? But he did not have to knock, after all.

Heavy footfalls came from somewhere inside, and a night-lock was turned; and there stood Schumacher with his vast confident smile.

"I heard you on the step, Frank."

The incarnation of certitude, Schumacher, as in his younger days; but now he looked at you longer and more closely, absorbing rather than dismissing you. He took Loring's hat as if confiscating it. "Nancy's lying down in the living room," Schumacher said. "This seems to be one of her bad evenings."

"Bad evenings?" Loring hardly ever had known that little romp to be ill.

"Oh, your coming will help to bring her round," Schumacher went on. "Yes, Frank, she's not been well for some time. The doctor hasn't a notion of the cause. But then, between you and me, what do M.D.'s know, eh? Not half what certain people I could name have got hold of—not a tenth!"

Yet Schumacher, when Loring had known him formerly, had been a complacent positivist. Changes in the fellow, yes—but the complacency remained. "You sound as if you'd been reading those Rosicrucian advertisements, Schumacher," Loring commented, meaning to be jocular. But the jocosity was punctured by a long heavy look from Schumacher. Schumacher condescending to be resentful?

"I don't mean quackery," Schumacher said. "Well, we'll go in to Nancy." He rapped perfunctorily at a door and pushed it open.

Nancy—ah, Nancy. The girl by the lake was in her yet. She had lain on a chaise longue, her little feet bare, as had been her fashion; and in her light green summer frock, supple and poised, she was for the moment Madame Récamier. But she rose quickly, gliding into neat slippers, and reached out both hands: "Oh, Frank!"

Loring flushed, almost giddy, as he took her hands. His shy smile, which Nancy and a few others could evoke, betrayed, he supposed, the interminable dreary story of his past ten years. And Nancy apprehended at once, he could tell—how observant she always was, and how quick they both had been to grasp each other's moods, back there before the Great Fact—yes, apprehended that he was not cured and had no hope of cure. She gave him a glance, quick and compassionate (was there something more than compassion in it?), and then swept her look on to her husband.

"We'll pull up by the bay window, eh?" said Schumacher, easily. When Nancy turned toward a big armchair, Schumacher gave her his hand, and Loring understood with a sudden pain that she needed it. Below her blue eyes were faint circles, and she was slim, all too slim, though youthful and fine skinned still. Her eyes glowed tonight; but, despite that, she was pale, weak and pale. She put Loring upon a plump stool at one side of her—"You always used to choose the stool, Frank, at every party, and I've been saving this one for you"—and Schumacher in a chair on her other side. Thus they sat and talked, Frank and Nancy, and natty, broad-shouldered, merry-dog Schumacher.

And every smile that Loring gave Nancy was a reflection of past folly; and every civility from her was an humiliation; and there was nothing they could say to each other that did not hurt. They talked of fripperies, college gossip, and sweltering summers and new books and tolerable restaurants. It was torment. Schumacher dominated—patronizing, self satisfied, full of talk. Schumacher was no bore: he talked much better than Loring had expected, and he listened to you when you had something to say—at least, he watched you, meeting your eyes with an absorbed and absorbing stare. No longer content with a physical triumph, did Schumacher want to dominate your mind? Even his efforts to put you at ease were disconcerting. Or had the sight and sound of Nancy shaken Loring's nerves?

To nerves, indeed, Schumacher presently led the conversation. Certainly no positivism remained in Schumacher. A startling blend of psychiatry and quasi-Yoga, spiced with something near to necromancy and perhaps a dash of Madame Blavatsky—this Schumacher's new system appeared to be. And this emitted by a swaggering professor of Spanish, late a disciple of the mechanists! Well, the line of demarcation between the two cults perhaps was no more difficult to cross than the boundary between Fascism and Communism, Loring reflected—but kept the observation private. How was Schumacher fetching Nancy into all this?

She had been leaning back in her chair with the polite air of a woman who has heard her husband too often on certain themes; but as Schumacher introduced her name, she sat up briskly, tucking her feet beneath her, and she listened with a fixity that set Loring wondering.

". . . waves of mind," Schumacher was saying. "Take Nancy: I'm sure no one suffers from a more subtle neurosis. It has to be the work of influences, waves of impulse, from origins and purposes we can only guess at—and not many of us are qualified to guess. *Neurosis* is an abused and misleading word, you understand, Frank. But there's almost no physical cause for Nancy's trouble—only physical effects.

What's the source, the impulse, eh? Where does it come from? What *wills* it?"

"The only trouble with me is, I'm sick," declared Nancy, with that humorous defiance Loring had known so long ago. "Something just ails my insides, that's all, Godfrey. I'm not the sort of girl that has the jitters, am I, Frank? I never was, was I?"

Swallowing, Loring said, "You were cool as the center seed of a cucumber, Nancy." Did she want to make him cry?

"You'd best take the doctors' word on that, hadn't you, dear?" Schumacher interrupted. "Three doctors we've called in, Frank. And what did they say, Nancy?"

Nancy crossed her arms pertly:

> "They cried in accents drear,
> 'There's nothing wrong with her!'"

"Well, not precisely that, dear," Schumacher admonished her, "now was it? As a matter of fact, Frank, they had to admit they simply didn't *know*. Loss of weight, loss of vitality, but no ascribable physical cause." Schumacher seemed positively to relish their bafflement. "'Waves of mind,' I told them. They couldn't follow me, of course—only M.D.'s. And they couldn't account for Nancy's dreams, either: a neurotic product quite outside their sphere, Loring—or Frank, that is. Tell Frank about your dreams, Nancy."

"Oh, other people's dreams are boring, aren't they, Frank?" She waved a little red-nailed hand. "And these are boring even to me, in a way, after so many nights of them. I'd better let sleeping mares lie."

"You can understand Nancy's not going into detail, Frank," said Schumacher, earnestly. "Dreadful sights, some of those visions of hers; glimpses that . . ."

Nancy cut him short, her full lips compressed in the imperious spirit Loring remembered too well: "My dreams, anyway, are my own, Godfrey. I hope you never have to share them. If you want an idea, a faint suggestion, of what they amount to, look at the pictures, Frank."

Loring had been vaguely conscious of a series of medium-sized colored prints, handsomely framed—four hung on each wall of the room—but until now his eyes had been all for Nancy. He rose and glanced at them. They were good prints: Breughel and Bosch and Teniers and Botticelli and a pair that Loring did not recognize. They were paintings of hell, every one, prints of those exquisitely horrid Flemish and German and Italian medieval-renaissance hells, their multitudinous tiny insect-devils flaying their innumerable little damned souls, their miniature burghs belching fire, their allegories of sin and unending torment expressed in sixteen ingenious diableries.

"*Deus misereatur*," murmured Loring, passing slowly from one picture to the next.

"Well, do you think my nerves have weakened with the years, Frank? Just how many wives could lie nearly all day in a room like this and not mind a bit?" She still had that naïve conceit of her courage. "I asked Godfrey why he couldn't let us have a touch of paradise, too; but no, he's set on his red devils."

"I didn't know you cared for this period," Loring observed to Schumacher.

Schumacher looked at him affably. "A man needs always

to be growing, finding new interests, new fields, you know. Art of this sort is one of my new ones. Cooking's another, by the way. What about it, dear?"

"I'm proud of Godfrey as a chef, since getting dinner became too much for me. He's done splendidly." Nancy spoke with a smiling seriousness. "Yes, you have, Godfrey."

"Apropos of that, it's time for coffee," Schumacher announced. "Coffee is one thing that Nancy can take and like, Frank. Eh, Nancy? It puts life into her, even gives her some appetite. A good nervous tonic, coffee. I'll have it ready in five minutes." And he went down the long corridor toward the kitchen, closing the doors behind him.

They looked at each other almost without expression, Nancy and Loring, alone for the first time since the Great Fact. Then Nancy said, "Give me your hand, Frank, and I'll show you something." He took her fragile hand, and she rose, and they went to a door on the nearer side of the room, and Nancy led him in. In a little bedroom, a boy of five or six was sleeping with a smile. "I can't remember when I slept like that," said Nancy, impassively. The boy was like Nancy, even to the long lashes. After a long look, Loring turned back to the living room, averting his face from Nancy.

"Frank, what's wrong?" she asked, with a tenderness that Loring had hoped to forget. He faced her, in an anger of sorts.

"You know, you know," Loring said. "He might have been mine."

She threw up her chin and looked him in the eyes, just the hint of tears above her lower lashes. "Yes"—defiantly—"and why not? Because you never really fought."

"What should I have done?" he asked, with his slow, sad smile. "Kicked you downstairs or locked you in a closet? You were willful then."

"Oh, I suppose there was nothing you could have done, Frank." She spoke now without resentment. "You simply weren't meant to win battles."

"I don't think I'm a coward, Nancy."

"No, no—I mean that you're too just and too slow. I like you for it, Frank; I love you for it; but it won't do in this world. You never truly fought for me."

"I'd fight now."

"Yes, when the victor's carried off the spoils. Frank, I'm glad you came, ever so glad; but what possessed you to come here?"

He was surprised. "Your husband said you wanted me."

"Frank, I didn't know you were coming until you knocked at this door; Godfrey never said he had asked you. I didn't know whether you were alive."

"I suppose he asked me to be polite," Loring reflected, "or perhaps because he thought I might perk you up."

"We always did make each other laugh, didn't we, Frank? No, Godfrey's thoughtful of me, but not in just that way; and he's not a polite man. What got into him, Frank?"

"He said you spoke of me often."

"Oh, I do, Frank! I've thought of you more as the years have slipped by, not less. I suppose I've spoken of you *too* often. Because Godfrey wouldn't understand what you and I were to each other. He's not made that way. He's lucky not to have sensibilities of that sort, probably. He's resented you, poor Godfrey. Now what's at the back of his head? Does he want to see what you're made of?"

"There's no cause for him to be jealous of me, Nancy, if he's thinking of the past. You never loved me as I hoped you might. But is he very jealous—in general?"

"Possessive is the better word for it. Oh, I shouldn't tell you this, Frank, but I always used to tell you everything. Yes, possessive. We don't see many people; he says he needs only me. Do you know, he doesn't much like my little boy, though he pretends to, because Johnny owns part of me. Godfrey wants all my time now, and all my future. I guess I ought to be grateful that anyone cares so much for me. And Godfrey wants my past—that, too, Frank. He's forever trying to assimilate my past, to take it away from me and make it his own. And I don't intend him to succeed. You're in my past, for one thing. He wants to know every little bit of it—when I had my first date, what boy was the first to kiss me. Poor Godfrey! He's longing to know more about you, and he won't believe there isn't any more to tell except what he couldn't understand. But he's been patient, ever so patient, since I've been sick. He waits on me, he reads to me. He watches me all the time. He calls in different doctors. He asks everybody's opinion of what ought to be done about me. Godfrey's a perfect nuisance, but a woman wants her husband to be that."

Loring shut his eyes, and said, "There's more to Godfrey than I'd expected."

"Meaning—"

"Meaning, for instance, these pictures on the wall."

"Yes—don't they give you the creeps, Frank? That's not all: he reads the most curious things, like the Kabbala, and *Satan's Wonderful World Unveiled*, and pamphlets on Cagliostro."

"Are you afraid of him, Nancy?"

"Afraid? You know I'm not afraid of any man born of woman." She reached out from her chair and gave Loring a playful push. "But men in dreams, now . . ."

"Still harping on dreams, you people?" Schumacher pushed through the doorway with a tray, and on it an oriental coffeepot of copper and little triangular sandwiches. "Dreams are manifestations of will. The dreamer's will, or another's. And if the will's strong enough, who knows where substance begins and ends? Eh, Frank?"

"I never had enough strength of will to bother."

"Is that really so?" Schumacher asked, with his stare of absorption. "You ought to exercise what will is in you, Frank, for you never can tell when it may have to put up a fight. Now here's your coffee, dear, and there's more where it came from. And yours, Lor—Frank. And mine with the cream in it."

Strong, strong, that coffee, sweetish and thick, almost Turkish. "An interesting blend," Loring remarked. "I think I like it. Your secret brew, Godfrey?"

"All in the grinding," Schumacher told him, with a satisfied little smile. "We have our own little mill here; and like the gods', it grinds slow and exceeding fine. Here, I'll fill your cup again, Nancy. What, no more for you, Frank? Come on, old man—one more cup. I'll be offended. That's better. Nancy can drink this stuff all night; it seems to rouse her."

So it did. With some of her old liveliness, Nancy stirred in her chair; her color heightened; she seemed the only cool thing in the hot night air. "I want to play matching lines," she told them. "Remember how we used to play it when we made lemonade, Frank, and sat on the porch? But it's always coffee for us now, even on nights like this: Godfrey's so proud of his coffee. It *is* good, Godfrey. Well, let's play. You won't be so good at this as Frank and I, Godfrey, because you went to a progressive school and didn't have to memorize. But you start, anyway."

Schumacher did not hesitate long. With a kind of sneer at the whole affair:

" 'No longer mourn for me when I am dead . . .' "

"Oh, a Shakespearean sonnet!"—this from Nancy. Loring remembered—

" 'Than you shall hear the surly sullen bell
Give warning to the world that I am fled
From this vile world, with viler worms to dwell.' "

"Ugh!" cried Nancy. "I like the next better:

" 'Nay, if you read this line, remember not
The hand that writ it; for I love you so
That I in your sweet thoughts would be forgot
If thinking on me then should make you woe.' "

"The surly sullen bell," Schumacher repeated, relishingly. "Not badly put—no, not bad. More coffee, Nancy, dear? Oh, yes—you need it."

With her clever little head, Nancy won the match. "She laughs as she always laughed," Loring thought, "no silly giggle." And this night he must go from her, back to that narrow hotel room with its silence. That girl! Well, he'd best go now. "It's been a good evening," he said to Schumacher, rising. Despite everything, he had no need to tell Nancy so.

At the door, Nancy took his hands again. "How long will it be before you come round, Frank?"

"February."

"You'll come here every night you're in town that week, won't you?" She meant it.

"If you'll have me."

"That's the old spirit!" Schumacher put in, loudly. He gripped Loring's hand powerfully. "Don't get lost on your way home, Frank. Sleep tight."

When Loring turned the corner, they still were watching him from their lighted doorway—a high, arrogant head, a little dear one. Ah, Nancy. "I never fought," Loring said, half aloud.

* * *

Now that the intoxication of Nancy's company ebbed away, Loring felt himself fallen into a solitude more oppressive than any grief he had known those past ten years. Quite literally the mood weighed upon him: his steps seemed weighted and painful, his eyes dim, his hearing dulled. He was aware of the fitful, warm night breeze only vaguely. And in this state Loring made his way through the district of ruined and ruinous old houses. Although he liked walking, tonight he would have whistled to a taxi, if any cab had passed; but it was late, and drivers knew they would have few fares in this slum.

Passing a building with its façade half battered in, so that broken plaster and lath were scattered over the ground by the slum children, Loring made out, a few yards ahead, another walker in this silent night, or rather morning. No third person appeared in the whole length of the street. A hulking figure, the other traveller's, and yet elusive, slipping now and again into deep shadow. For the better part of a block the other man preceded Loring—and then was gone.

Loring blinked sleepily. Gone where? He came up to the spot where he had lost sight of the other walker, and observed a filthy little alley leading to the right. Acting upon some subtle impulse, Loring turned into the alley, and in a moment found himself at the entrance to a decrepit court, strewn with old tin cans and heaped cinders, and faced by the grim backs of four or five condemned houses. There was no one to be seen. And whatever was he doing here? Why had he left the road? Loring went back to the street, and a quarter of an hour later was unlocking the door of his hotel room.

Dreams came to him that night, a series of hopeless longings and dissolving frights impossible to recollect long after waking, but sufficient to rouse him, crying out, three times in the dark. And when he got out of bed in the morning, something was wrong: a complaint like acute rheumatism combined with extreme lethargy. Loring had to eat breakfast in his room, and the elevator boy saved him from slipping as he got heavily out upon the ground floor to go about his business. All day he was in some strong discomfort, and the next day, too, and in diminishing measure for three weeks after; but then he drifted back into his old careless good health. Ah, Nancy, Loring thought—what you do to me even now.

* * *

In February, St. Louis covers its snow with grime and dust, bad as tar and feathers. Underneath, that snow was nearly two feet deep when Loring went to make his call upon the Schumachers, for the seething heat of his last visit had given way to the rigor of a continental winter. Loring stamped his feet and pulled off his galoshes on Schumacher's steps, and this brought Schumacher to the door without Loring's having to knock.

"Nancy's dozing," said Schumacher, quietly. "We'll sit in the living room—she's there—and she'll wake gradually. This is the only sort of sleep she gets now. Far gone, Frank, far gone: the doctors haven't the ghost of a notion of what to do. Now and then her appetite returns, though. I watch her every moment I'm at home." He stared at Loring as if challenging the sincerity of Loring's condolences.

That bewitched and bewitching girl! Madame Récamier as before, she opened her eyes to Loring, smiled, and whispered, "Six months? I thought you had been away six centuries, Frank." She did not attempt to rise, and she was pale, pale as paper and nearly as thin, though the loveliness had not gone out from her.

"I love you more than ever, Nancy," was what Loring wished to say. Instead, he had to sit and talk follies with this shadow of the girl by the lake and with this elegant bull of a man. After a time, their conversation shifted somehow to Ends. Nancy was responsible for it, probably, and she said in her faint, piquant voice that she was inclined to believe the End was in another world altogether, this one being only a means of purging.

"Another world? Why, there's your other world for almost everybody," Schumacher broke in, gesturing toward the holy terrors on the wall. "Right there you can see both this life and the next. Only spiritual power can snatch you out of that trap. Not one man in a hundred thousand has that kind of power."

"If you were right, then I'd see if I couldn't leave behind me something decent to be remembered by, anyhow," Loring retorted. "A name for honesty, or honest children."

Schumacher was vehemently contemptuous. "What's the significance of a name when there's no one to pat you on the back?"

Then what was Schumacher's End? Loring inquired.

"Spiritual triumph." Schumacher leaned forward with a glare of conviction that made Loring shift uneasily. "I don't subscribe in the least to the Hebrew-Christian myth, you understand: I mean actuality, the exultation of battles won in the most dangerous of fields, the spirit plane. In the spirit realm there's no time; the fight goes on forever; you must be always on guard; and you trample down the beaten. That's what all this"—sweeping a hand toward St. Louis, outside in the dark—"is for, and all that," motioning toward the Breughels and Bosches. "They're both veils for the real plane of being. And in that hard reality you survive and progress by conquest. Oh, you can't comprehend my meaning till you've reached that plane. You need to dominate, to crush . . ." Abruptly Schumacher became casual again. "Which reminds me, I'd better grind the coffee." He went into the kitchen.

Nancy glanced up at Loring with a small smile, half quizzical, half appealing. "What do you make of Godfrey, Frank?"

An awkward question to answer. "I'd never have suspected him, in the old days, of a mystical turn."

"It's because he's a disappointed man, Frank. He's turned to these ideas since he realized he's not going far in this world." So faint, her voice, and yet so calm.

"Godfrey's done well enough."

"Frank, you don't know him! He thought he was meant to be Alexander, and instead he's a professor of languages. Godfrey's ever so vain, or was. And yet he can't even contrive to become a dean; and *that's* no lofty triumph in these days, Lord knows. He's big, he's clever, he's handsome, he works hard; but there's not enough in him. He simply doesn't get ahead; and in spite of all his efforts, not many people like him. He knows these things now. So he's stopped trying in everyday life, Frank—'in this plane,' he'd say—and he's seeing what *will* can do. He never loved anyone but himself, and now he detests the whole world because people won't permit him to own them."

"Does he hate you, Nancy?" It was all Loring could manage to force that question out.

"Yes; but more than ever he wants to possess me, absorb me, lose me in himself. He married the wrong sort of wife for that. He should have chosen a meek girl, submissive and infinitely loving, shouldn't he? I've the love, perhaps, but not one ounce of meekness. I'd lose myself in him if I could, but it's not my way: I'm too *alive*, Frank. Even now, a bag of bones, there's too much life in me to be assimilated to Godfrey. He detests me because he can't swallow me whole. I loved him ten years ago because he wanted to swallow me; while you hardly dared say 'Boo!' to Nancy. In a way, I love him now."

Loring pulled his chair closer to the chaise longue. She always had been slim; and tonight it seemed as if the faintest breeze would sweep her up. "What are we going to do about you, Nancy?" Now that he saw her pale face so close, he bit his lip.

"Frank, you're *good*. Don't think I'm a shadow because I want to end everything: I've matters to live for. I don't know what's wrong and I suppose I never will know. The sun doesn't help, or change of diet, or sleep—when I manage to sleep. Godfrey doesn't spare money in trying to help me, you understand. He never was mean about anything, least of all his wife. It just seems to be destined, Frank. The end might come this hour, or it might be next year. I'm not afraid, either."

"I'd be afraid, darling," Loring told her. "Don't speak to me of death."

"Whom else am I to speak to? Whom did I always trust? I try to talk with Godfrey about—about my prospects; but he only laughs, to turn such talk away. Laughs at a dying woman! It's hard to forgive him that opinion of my intelligence, for I know he tells everyone else about the dreadful shape I'm in. Gossip drifts back. I'm telling you, Frank, because this may be our last minute to ourselves. I want to say that I'm sorry I never was more to you. I'm sorry you see me like this, and not the way I used to be; but oh, I'm glad you came."

Loring's breath came hard. In the kitchen a cup fell and

smashed; they could hear Schumacher rearranging the coffee-tray.

"And there's one thing I ask you, Frank, though I have no right: look out for my little boy."

"He has a father, Nancy girl."

"I asked you to look out for my little boy, Frank." She reached for his hand. "Johnny's like me."

"You know I will." Then Loring bent and kissed her, and went in a daze to the window, with his back toward Nancy—and only just in time, if that, for Schumacher was entering with the coffee.

"There you are, Nancy dear—thick, the way you like it. Not too hot for you, is it, Frank? Don't let it cool long: heat's half the secret of flavor. There's more as soon as you've drunk that."

If conceivable, stronger and more like a syrup than it had been six months before, Schumacher's coffee. "I prefer your coffee to your philosophy," said Loring, huskily.

"What's your objection?" Schumacher turned upon him that zealot's stare.

"For one thing, your doctrine of 'spiritual triumph' is the rejection of morality."

"Morality?" Schumacher waved a big hand. "Well, if we must bring the subject up, you've heard what William James said about morality: 'So long as one poor cockroach feels the pangs of unrequited love, this world is not a moral world.' Morality is the satisfaction of desire."

"So the more successful the thief, the better man he is?" Loring asked.

Nancy, roused somewhat by the coffee, smiled her approval of Loring's bluntness. "Morality's restraint," she said.

"No, restraint is for spiritual weaklings," Schumacher insisted. "Strength is everything upon the physical plane, and that's just as true, really, upon the spiritual—the moral—plane. Strength and appetite are the only tests. You'll admit that soon enough, Loring." He refilled Loring's cup.

Loring hung on that night until he could not postpone, in decency, saying goodbye. When there was nothing else left to do, he took Nancy's hand, and they two exchanged a long look. "Frank, remember me," said pallid Nancy. Loring kept a grip upon himself.

She could not go with him to the door, but Schumacher did. They shook hands upon the steps. "You've seen her, Frank, so you know she hasn't long." Schumacher grimaced. "She might go tomorrow, or next week, for all we can tell. It's best you came tonight."

"I'll come by tomorrow evening, too, if I may," Loring answered.

"Tomorrow? Oh, yes—try to stop by, if you can."

Loring walked to the gate in the brick wall, opened it, began to turn into the street. At that instant he glimpsed Schumacher still watching him from the steps, staring intently, as if with his whole soul. His look was so fixed that Loring glared back. Then Schumacher, starting, jerked up his right hand in an awkward wave: "Well, goodbye . . . !" The words were bleated out in a high drawl. Loring left that big queer figure and went into the dark.

* * *

Lead was in Loring's soles. What had come over him? He felt a touch of vertigo. Every step had become a distinct effort, every swing of his body an ache. The snow crunched beneath his galoshes. As he approached the broken tenements of the Old Town, fresh snow commenced to fall heavily; and the wind came up, wailing through the empty windows, obscuring the other side of the street with white scurries swept from loose drifts. His eyes were heavy, his pulse was distressing, his breathing difficult; and he was alone in the cold.

Alone except for the one who walked there ahead of him. Loring felt a dull necessity, in his oppressive state, to seek company; and yet something made him reluctant to overtake the fellow ahead. Anyway, the other walker seemed to be slowing his pace. Now Loring was close to him, though the other remained indistinct amid the snowflakes. They both were passing the house of the smashed façade; the other walked a mere dozen steps in the lead. A minute later, Loring came abreast of the other.

Loring glanced into his face: a large face, smiling. But after some fashion the face did not live. And it was Schumacher's face.

Crying out, Loring leaped away from that face and blundered in an agony of confusion down the alley on the right. Slipping and reeling, he got through the drifts into the stinking little court of the condemned houses. He still had courage enough to look back, and there was nothing behind him. Recovered a bit, he crept up to the shelter of a house wall. But a face was peering from a window in the wall. It was Schumacher's face.

At that, Loring fell forward in the snow, and for some time experienced nothing.

But though he lay with his face in the drift, oblivious of the court around him and of the conscious world, soon the horrors came to him. Dreams compounded of the vilest frights, visions of torment unceasing, ecstasies of revulsion, went round and round and round. And out of the chinks and corners of these arabesques peered the eyes of Schumacher. Lie still, said whatever was left of Loring: lie still, hiding yourself in blackness. Slowly the merciful blackness crept through Loring's nerves. Through the grotesque terrors of his trance, some old Scottish epitaph pounded with lunatic insistency through his twilight consciousness:

> "When the last trump shall sound,
>   And the dead shall rise,
> Lie still, Red Rab,
>   If ye be wise."

And still Loring would have lain. But presently other eyes emerged from behind the arabesques of damnation. And these other eyes were Nancy's. "You never really fought, you never really fought." The sentence flitted without meaning among the arabesques, and Schumacher's eyes peeked out once more. Ah, to hide with Red Rab in the blackness! Yet something held him. With an immense effort, he compelled the arabesques to halt in their dance for a moment. In their place came a glimpse of Nancy, lying upon her couch. "My little boy . . ." The terrors thrust themselves back upon Loring; but a thought, a fragment of consciousness, had intruded among them. Some wild struggle of will, or wills, was fought out then, lasting only seconds, perhaps, but seeming aeons. And abruptly Frank Loring sat up in the snow.

He opened his eyes, the bravest act of his life. The

shattered window of the tenement confronted him, and the face of Schumacher was in it still, and Loring wailed shrilly. Yet Loring stared on, and in time Schumacher's face seemed to dissolve into its constituent atoms, and Loring was looking merely into an empty ruin.

Then Loring got up from the drift. He got up with strong pain and difficulty, for the sake of Nancy's memory. "You never really fought." He rose, his will awake, and groped along the brick walls to the street. "My little boy . . ." He had lain a long time in the snow, and seemed frozen.

And though he was weak as water, and giddy beyond belief, and incapable of speech, he lurched and crept four blocks to a police station. The few people he passed took him for a stumblebum. He pushed his way into the station; and there, in the overheated room, lounged four of the tough, weary policemen of St. Louis. One of these started to say, "Get the hell—." Then, looking at Loring, he came forward to take his arm, and asked uncertainly, "What's up, fellow?"

"I've been poisoned," said Loring. He gave Schumacher's name and address, and then fell, dead weight, into a sergeant's arms.

*   *   *

When the police came to his door, Godfrey Schumacher went upstairs and shot himself, so that no questions ever were asked of him. Downstairs at the time was a doctor, certifying that heart failure had been the cause of the death, that night, of Nancy Schumacher. Presently this verdict was altered to "poisoning from a strychnic preparation, administered in increasing quantities over a considerable period of time"—after Loring had talked with the coroner. But neither Loring nor the doctors ever knew more, and Loring suspected that their "strychnic" was little better than approximation.

"Frank, remember me." Ay, thou pale ghost, while memory holds a seat. And looking upon the little boy, Loring saw the bones, the mouth, the impish eyes of her for whom he had not fought until the last second of her life.

THE CELLAR OF LITTLE EGYPT

♩

"Where will we all be a hundred years from now?
Where will we all be a hundred years from now?
Pushing up the daisies, pushing up the daisies:
That's where we'll all be a hundred years from now."

The other morning I heard the little scamps across the street singing this, and it set me to thinking of Uncle Jake and Amos Trimble. You don't believe there's anything in a town like New Devon but asphalt pavements and supermarkets. Well, grow to be an old codger here, the way I have, and you'll come to know that life's as much a puzzle in New Devon as it is anywhere. And folks remember things they don't tell children. . . . But I'll tell you about Amos Trimble, as my Uncle Jake told me. That'll do for a sample.

When I was little we had eight shoemakers in town. Fifty years gone; but it could be a thousand, for the difference in New Devon. Eight shoemakers in town then, and nowadays never a one left. That old way of living was strangled by the factories and the cars. North along the river road, beginning where the town dump is now and stretching on for miles, were good farms—farms of the kind you can't find in the whole county these days. Look at the Millard place, what's left of it, and you'll have a notion. Most of the others are gone, every scrap of them, the square brick houses with cupolas, and carriage barns behind them, and scale houses. Next to the dump, you can see the foundation of one of the biggest: the house where Amos Trimble lived, and afterward—but that's another matter.

It's hard to think of New Devon without mills. On the south side you see as many smokestacks as I saw barns on the river road, when I used to steal my Uncle Jake's plug tobacco. Where the tube mill stands, Amos Trimble used to drive that surrey of his through the short cut to Little Egypt. A little red scar was over Mr. Trimble's right eye, that touched his eyelid and wrinkled if he looked sidewise at you; but he didn't often look at me—he wasn't the sort that boys ask pennies from.

Eight shoemakers, then; and Uncle Jake was one. The three of us, his nephews, used to sit in his shop, watching him nailing down soles. He'd put a nail where he wanted it, and raise the hammer, and pound three times. "Hum, hum, hum!" he'd say; and when it went home, "Hum, b'God!" When he wasn't looking, we'd stick his tobacco in our pockets. Jake was in his thirties, but he seemed like an old man to us; and he was old, too. Turning away from the liquor made a change in him, and keeping off the bottle took nerve for a man who belonged to my family. But from the day Dan Slattery died downstairs in Little Egypt, Jake wouldn't look at booze.

We had a different kind of men in New Devon those

days. Could they work! But, then, that's all there was for them—work, or else drink. Never a day without a real fight—half of them at Little Egypt. No movies, no lodges, no women in barrooms—nothing but work and whiskey. The men were devils for both. After he had to leave the liquor, Uncle Jake could only work. You never see a man, these days, drive himself the way Jake did. He didn't leave himself time to think. There'd been a day when people called him a great reader—before he got in with the boys at Little Egypt. I suppose he'd have been happier if he had been a fool. Maybe that was why he loved the whiskey: it made a fool of him. When he was sober he thought of what he'd like to be and never could—too slow for the turf, too light for the plow. And so he was drunk all his life, first on rot-gut, then on work.

You and I have got our feet on the ground. Sometimes that's an advantage; sometimes not. There are things we miss. A dog hears sounds a man can't; a fellow like Jake who hasn't got his feet on the ground, who's drunk and weak and maybe a little off—why, how can you or I judge what they see or feel, these fellows, or how much truth they make out through a whiskey-fog? I don't know. Jake was no fool, and I think he never lied. He was drunk on the day Slattery died, and he wasn't afraid, much; but as he thought about it afterward, he froze. Nobody could get him to touch a body, after that time in the cellar of Little Egypt.

Most of what I know about this I learned from Jake one afternoon in his shop—Jake sitting cross-legged on the bench, a shoe half finished in his lap, his little blue eyes (hard as marbles) looking past me toward the window, as if he wanted to see who might peer in. Jake was cold sober when he told me, and had been that way for years.

My Uncle Jake was the first man in New Devon to see Amos Trimble. I think he was the last to see him, too. On a fall morning, Jake said, a square-built, bearded man, who might have been almost forty or might have been younger, came off the train from Detroit and put his bag on the cinders beside the depot. Along the railway siding New Devon was no beauty spot, even then; and I don't suppose Jake made it prettier—leaning against the depot, rough looking as they come, and needing a shave, as always. The man from off the train looked round as if he were saying, "I'd straighten this up, fast," and then eyed Jake. Jake wasn't the kind to kowtow to God Almighty, so he kept on leaning; but he said to me, there in the shop, "Roy, that fellow made me squirm. He had green eyes that looked right into your damned rotten heart."

"Well, sir," said the stranger to Jake, "I'm Amos Trimble, and I'm looking for the Devon House." Jake stood up, though he wasn't naturally obliging, and nodded:

"All right, Mr. Trimble; I can take a walk that way." When they got to the Devon House, Trimble stood Jake a drink. Amos Trimble was a drinking man, Jake said; but he was stone sober, all the same, day or night. "Frightening collected, all the time," were the words Jake used, "except when he wanted to make you laugh. He could split your sides if he had a mind to. Fact is, he could make anybody do anything." Jake took to him, right away, though Jake didn't care for many people.

Trimble came to New Devon from the West. Whether he had been born out there, he didn't say; and nobody asked Amos Trimble questions like that. I don't mean that Trimble had a Past, in the usual way of speaking. He lived his own life, that was all, and it may not have been happy. He could tell you stories for hours, but they weren't stories about himself. He was honest straight through, and when he told you to lick dirt, you licked. It leaked out that he had been a lumberman and a land speculator and a judge of probate; and now he was going to stay in New Devon, where he had bought a farm for himself and was going to buy and sell the farms of other people. He had some money and was likely to have more. Only the cellar hole is there by the dump, now, but what was the Adams place—the oldest big house in the township—was grand when Trimble came to New Devon, and he bought it. He made it his house right away, and it stayed Amos Trimble's house, even after he was gone, until it burned. Trimble cut his mark deep on everything. He lived alone; his tenants across the road took care of the farm. That house came to look like Trimble, square and shaggy and proud.

At Little Egypt, the boys didn't know what to make of Mr. Trimble—Dan Slattery and Jack Cane and Red Fellows and the rest. Cane thought he was a man to steer clear of; Fellows said Cane was yellow; and the two of them tangled about it one afternoon till Mrs. Johnston, who owned Little Egypt, had to come downstairs with a broom and get them both outside, her black wig falling off as she shoved them through the doorway, showing her old bald head to everybody at the depot. Where the Hotel Puritan is today, that's where Little Egypt stood. Sixty years before, it had been a first-rate tavern, one of the prettiest in the state; I've got a snapshot of it, taken the year they tore it down. Downstairs was a good solid taproom, and above that six or seven sleeping rooms; it had columns along the second story, facing the street, like the Millard place. But when Mrs. Johnston, old Baldy Johnston, ran it, it was a filthy hole. It had been named the Madison, but after some of the boys went to the Exposition at Chicago, they called the saloon Little Egypt, because it was as free as that dancing girl in '92. In Baldy Johnston's time there was still a long oak bar, and Slattery was behind it.

Bloody Dan, my brothers and I used to call him after looking round to make sure he wasn't down the alley. Six feet four, almost, and built for it. He'd been a butcher, and liked the work, but he got free drinks behind the bar at Little Egypt. It was something curious to watch him knock a cow between the eyes or slit a pig's throat—one knock, one slice, and all over. Blood was slopped on him most days, since he butchered for Smith now and then even after he was hired by Baldy Johnston. At Little Egypt nobody minded a barkeeper with a little blood on him. It wasn't safe to mind Dan, anyway. He had more cunning in him than you'd think, to look at his big empty face with all the front teeth missing. Dan was an animal, with a beast's quickness and a beast's suspicions.

As for Red Fellows, he was a rough customer who'd crippled his mother with a couple of kicks one night after he lost his shirt at poker. Jack Cane, who stuck with them, had served time for stealing; he was mostly muscle. Jake used to play cards with them a good deal—he was one man that dared to.

And Amos Trimble—it's odd enough—was in and out of Little Egypt some days. He seemed to have a liking for a bit of rough company. Good at poker, Trimble, as at everything; and even Bloody Dan forked over when he lost to him. I don't suppose Dan loved him, though.

But it was only some evenings that you could find Mr. Trimble at Little Egypt. Other times, he'd stick among the books at his old square house, his kerosene lamp burning all night. He read a lot, that was clear; but other nights, Jake thought, Trimble must have sat from sundown to sunup in his high leather chair, not moving, not reading, staring into some corner. He wasn't a man you could kid. Brice, the undertaker, came on business one evening, and found Trimble that way, sitting straight and solemn, his eyes open but not blinking. Brice had to shake Mr. Trimble two or three times before he stirred; and when he did wake, or speak, the whites of his eyes showed with anger, though he was polite enough, and Brice wished he never had touched him. A queer duck, in a fine house; but the house was dark and musty with only Trimble there. Jake said it would have given him the creeps to live in it alone; he got a look at the place the day he went with Brice and George Russell (who was deputy sheriff) to tell Amos Trimble what had happened to Jingo Criminy. When you needed any sort of help, Trimble was the man to look to. Russell needed it, and he remembered that Trimble had been a judge. They came up through the deep snow that covered the steps, that January, and Trimble led them to the upstairs parlor, and they told him about Jingo Criminy. It had been a dull winter in New Devon, until then.

What Jingo Criminy's real name was doesn't matter. "Well, by Jingo Criminy!" the dirty old man would say, whether he'd taken in another dollar or dropped his glass eye. Jingo had lived alone in his cabin across the river for twenty years and more, and he didn't spend much on himself. The dollars came in, slowly, and Jingo Criminy hid them away. In twenty years, a heap of silver dollars can go into a box. There must have been a good many men in New Devon who thought about those dollars, because it was three miles from Jingo's cabin to town. Three men thought too long.

How did Jake know there were three? No, he wasn't one, for Jake had a heart; but talk comes out. There were three of them, and they took a cutter: three big men, faces hard as the ice on the road, and it was cold—too cold for anybody else to be out that evening. The snow crunched under the runners, and they came to Jingo's cabin, and they broke down the door. Crazy old coots like Jingo don't talk, even with matches at their feet, but sometimes they talk when they're strapped to the stove. Maybe Jingo Criminy talked, and maybe they found the hole in the floor without his help. They tore up the boards and emptied the box and went away in the cutter; but when they went, they left Jingo Criminy still strapped to the stove. A couple of days later, someone noticed the cabin door open, and looked in.

That meant a job for Uncle Jake. Brice was a good undertaker, but there were times when he needed help, and Jake was his man. Nothing turned Jake's stomach, which was cast iron. He and Brice took old Jingo off the stove, while Russell stood by; and as soon as they could, they went to Trimble's. Nothing was known, then, about the cutter and the three men, you understand: the snow had melted part way down, so there were no tracks.

If anybody knew men, Trimble did. Deputy Russell came

to him for that and for something more. You could see that Trimble had power; some people said that he had powers. Russell believed in powers. Those were the big years for the spiritualists. Russell believed in the whole kit and kaboodle, and nobody thought he was queer. Trimble didn't take too much stock in it, Jake said. Could he see things, though—things afar off, or done in the past? Yes, sometimes, Trimble told them. He would try. They sat in the dark of the upstairs parlor with their fingers pressed hard on the table top. Jake was across from Trimble. The sight of Jingo hadn't turned a hair of Jake's head, but Trimble's green eyes two feet away behind the candle flame was a sight he didn't like. For five minutes they sat, till Trimble's voice said, "They tied him with his face to the stove."

"That's true, Mr. Trimble," Russell whispered. "What about *their* faces?"

Amos Trimble stood up and lit the gas; Jake saw sweat running down his forehead. "That's no evidence for you—not yet," Trimble said. "I'll see what I can find. I'm going to Little Egypt, once I write this note." He scribbled something while Jake and the rest were getting on their coats, and tucked it away. "I'll see you tonight, Mr. Russell," he said. But he didn't.

Trimble had faith in himself, as he had a right to. Something slipped that evening—Jake never knew what; but for once, Trimble failed himself. He didn't make the mistake twice.

Down to Little Egypt Trimble went; and Jake, being thirsty and curious, went with him. Fellows and Cane and a couple of boomer switchmen were near the bar, Slattery and a helper behind it. Baldy Johnston was sick abed upstairs that day. One of the switchmen called Jake over for a drink, while Trimble walked halfway round the bar and looked at Slattery. There wasn't the man who could help being stared down by Amos Trimble.

"Well?" asked Dan. Nothing happened. "Well, Mr. Trimble?" For him, Trimble was the only Mister in town, and he must have hated Trimble for it.

"What's roasting today, Slattery?" Trimble said. A vein swelled across Dan's forehead; he opened his mouth wide, but no words came.

Red Fellows, for once, thought faster than Dan. "What do you say to a game, Mr. Trimble?" Fellows edged closer, till Trimble looked sidewise at him, the little scar on his eyelid puckering, then Fellows shifted back.

"I'll play your game," said Amos Trimble.

"Let's go in the back room, then," growled Dan, who hadn't quite got his breath back. Trimble nodded and motioned to the three to go in ahead of him; he shook his head at Jake, who had started to rise; and then Trimble closed the door behind himself. Jake heard chairs scraping up to the table and made out Dan's voice every few minutes—whining first, then hoarse. But Jake had other fish to fry, because the boomer switchman was in the cash and the drinks were on him. Even Jake had his limit for whiskey, and he went past it.

Something roused Jake of a sudden. How long had he been lying with his head on the table, alone? He didn't know. It was a breaking noise that woke him, he thought, and he shook his head. The boomer switchmen were gone; there was no light in the taproom. He could see light coming from under the door of the back room, though. He headed for it and turned the knob, but the door was bolted. Jake gave it a kick. Nobody spoke. "Come on!" said Jake, and nearly knocked a panel out. The door opened a crack, Dan showing his ugly face behind it. Jake gave him a shove and stepped in, nearly falling flat over the trap door to the cellar, which had been thrown open in the middle of the kitchen floor. Dan swore, and steadied Jake, who was blinking in the light. The room was empty except for Dan, who must have been washing, because water and suds were slopped over him. That surprised Jake a bit, soap not being in Dan's line.

"Where's Mr. Trimble and the rest?" Jake asked him.

"Gone home, long ago," was all Dan said, slamming down the cellar trap and standing upon it.

Jake still didn't know what had waked him, but he was willing to forget. He told Dan to give him another bottle. "Serve yourself," said Dan, pushing him out into the bar. Jake obliged, and finally put his head down on the table for a minute.

Jake woke again, and found he was lying on the porch of Little Egypt in the snow—nothing for Jake—and it was sometime in the early morning, and not a star out. Jake could walk, but he didn't feel like it. If Slattery had put him out, he'd try his luck with Slattery tomorrow. His bed was half a mile away. Just then, though, he heard a buggy coming out of the stable behind Little Egypt: a ride for him, maybe. Jake slipped down the steps and made for the corner of the tavern; just before he reached it, Amos Trimble's surrey, pulled by his smart bay, came into sight.

"How about a lift, Mr. Trimble?" called out Jake. The surrey moved on, the driver snuggled in a rug. "Hey, Mr. Trimble, it's Jake," Uncle Jake yelled. The bay started out at a brisk walk along the road beside the railway tracks. Jake stumbled and went into a drift; when he was up again, the surrey had gone round a turn. "What did I do tonight that Trimble doesn't speak?" thought Jake. It was a cold half-mile home.

And it still was cold next morning when Brice pulled Jake out of bed to give him another job. "A fellow got mixed up with a train at Tecumseh crossing, early today," said Brice. "That's what it looks like, though I can't figure out what train. He must have walked there—no sign of a horse. I don't know who. It's a mess, Jake; he's scattered for a hundred yards."

Tecumseh crossing was halfway between the New Devon depot and Trimble's farm. The man, or what had been one, was only patches in the snow, Jake told me. Jake went along carefully with a basket, picking up everything; when he worked, he earned his pay. He and Brice came to a boot; Brice looked at it and gave a moan: "Trimble's." Jake never talked much. "Can't be," he said. "Trimble's not the kind." Jake found the other boot. "Not his," he said, but he didn't look at it closely.

It was Jake, too, who came to the head, with the black beard all stiff, and, in spite of dirt and blood, the scar still clear over the right eye. "Oh, God, Mr. Trimble; oh, God, Mr. Trimble, not you," was all Jake could say that day. The surrey was in the stable at Little Egypt; Trimble hadn't been sober enough to drive, the people there said. And what was Jake's word? He'd been lying in the snow on the porch like a sick hog. Brice had to go on with the work alone. He found everything, at last, except one thumb.

* * *

What was done? What you'd expect, with no more to go on. Russell could talk to Slattery, but Dan had his story. Lacking proof, there was no point in rousing Slattery's gang, in the lonely winter, with Russell the only officer in town. Jake might have done something, if he hadn't been married to the bottle. As it was, he kept clear of Little Egypt most of the time.

And here is where I fit into the picture—though I didn't know it was a picture, at the time. Spring came early that year. Sam Johnston—Baldy Johnston's little boy—and I were like a couple of cubs out of a cave, and got to wrestling in the mud of the back yard of Little Egypt. Sam was fatter, and got me down, and bounced on me. Jake came along and looked at us. "What'll I do, Uncle Jake?" I asked him.

"If I was in your place, Roy," he said, "I'd eat my way out. Sam's nose is mighty close to you." Sam gave a yell, and jumped off, and Jake walked on. Both Sam and I had had enough, so we started to plague Baldy Johnston's old cat, which was in the yard with us.

The cat was playing with something when Sam pulled it by the tail. I grabbed the thing it had been pushing around. At first I didn't know what it was. But when I turned it over, I saw the nail. It was shrunken and dry, but it was a man's thumb. I let it drop.

Sam bawled for his mother. She came out and took a look at the thing; you wouldn't have thought much could upset Baldy Johnston, but she opened her mouth to scream and then stopped herself, white as a tablecloth. "Dan!" she screeched, instead. Dan stepped out of the taproom. His face didn't change. "That damned cat's been in the cellar," was all he said—all that I could make out. He muttered something else, lower, to Baldy.

"Why didn't you make sure?" said Baldy, furious.

"Don't worry," Dan told her. "The stove's hot." He picked up the thing in the dirt. Old Baldy shivered.

"No, you don't, Dan," she said. "Get a spade." She and Dan looked at us, and Sam and I made tracks out of there. Sam's mother must have taught him not to talk, and I didn't say anything. When I was a kid, I had nobody really to talk with, anyhow; and I was scared this time, though I didn't understand why.

It could have been evidence, but no one else knew. There was one other piece of proof somewhere, maybe: Russell thought of the note Trimble had scribbled at his house, before he went to Little Egypt the last time. Russell and Jake and Brice had seen him write something. But where had he put it? It wasn't in the clothes they found along the tracks, and it didn't turn up at the house. Nobody had any idea of what Trimble had written. Russell was ready to quit.

As the months went by, Jake drifted back to Little Egypt and drowned himself in Baldy Johnston's raw whiskey. One afternoon early in July, Jake was playing poker with Fellows and two other boozers—a rough game, with plenty of money on the table. Cane was at the bar, talking with Slattery. A lucky day for Jake. After three hands, everything went his way. Ordinarily he was a bad player; this day it seemed to him as if someone were looking over his shoulder and giving him tips, the queer feeling that gamblers sometimes have. All said, something peculiar hung about Little Egypt that afternoon. Jake always could feel what was in the air; and Slattery seemed to know something was odd, too, shifting back and forth behind the bar, spoiling for a fight.

Red Fellows never could take a licking at cards. When Jake threw down the deuce, he set up a howl: "What's going on, you midget? I already played the deuce." It was all wind, but both he and Jake were ready to make something of it; Little Egypt was on their nerves.

"The hell," said Jake, pushing back his chair and reaching for the money. "My deuce." Fellows picked up a big schooner of beer from the table and let fly at Jake's head.

Jake wasn't tall, but he was thick where it counted. The schooner scratched the red cap Jake wore. Jake reached across the table, hoisted Fellows up, spun him round, and let him fly into the front window. Fellows broke half a dozen bottles when he landed.

"If you're going to kill him, don't kill him in here," yelled Slattery, coming over the bar. Jake was sick of Slattery. He heaved a chair at Bloody Dan.

The chair missed Dan; it brushed a lighted lamp and knocked it on the floor. Dan went after Jake, but Jake was quick for a man of his build, and side-stepped. They sparred round the floor while Fellows crawled out of the window, pulling glass from his pants. Then they started to cough, and found they couldn't see to fight—the smoke was too thick. The lamp had set Little Egypt afire.

Flame in one corner, smoke everywhere. The two other

boys who'd been in the game got out the door and ran for help. Cane went for a bucket of water at the pump, and Jake and Fellows and Slattery tried smothering the flames with a couple of rag rugs. But it was old wood, Little Egypt. The fire spread, and all of a sudden an awful yowl came up from somewhere. "My God, who's that?" asked Jake, coughing harder. Slattery swung round, but Jake couldn't see his face for the smoke. The yowl came again, and someone opened the door of the backroom, though Jake couldn't make out who was coming in—Cane, probably.

"Hell, it's only the cat, scared silly down below," Fellows grunted, beating at the fire with a broom. He was at the far side of the room. "Get a move on with that water, Cane!"

But Jack Cane didn't come in. The backroom door swung to again; and someone said, through the smoke, "Why don't you get us out of the cellar, Slattery?" The closing of the door muffled whatever else was said, and Jake was too busy with his rug to pay much attention; but the voice was nothing like Cane's.

"Dan!" said Fellows. He had dropped his broom, and was leaning against the wall, too startled by something even to swear. "Dan, who was that? It sounded like . . ."

"Shut up, damn you," Dan told him; but he whispered it. Slattery was crouched in the middle of the floor, ignoring the fire, watching the backroom door. "I couldn't see a thing. It must of been Jack." The door did not open again.

"Come on, Dan!" howled Jake, who was getting hot, what with the fire gaining. "Grab that rug!" But Dan stood there, staring at the door. Jake beat at the fire; and then a crowd of section-hands ran in with buckets of water. Little Egypt had one inside wall burnt nearly through, but nothing worse. By the time Jake got the smoke out of his eyes, Dan and Fellows were standing outside by the porch, saying nothing but letting other people finish the fire. "Say, where's Cane?" asked Fellows, after a while.

They looked in the backroom, but found not hide nor hair of Jack Cane. Nobody in New Devon saw Cane from that time on. About two o'clock was the time the fire started in Little Egypt. At ten past two, the Detroit train came into New Devon. Just before it whistled—so Rowson, the ticket agent, told people—Cane ran into the depot and bought a ticket. He looked over his shoulder, and swore at Rowson for being slow, and grabbed his ticket and made the train. He didn't take anything with him. Why he went, nobody knew, and nobody ever had a chance to ask him. Two weeks later, Cane was dead in a rooming house in Chicago: some said bad liquor, some said carbolic acid. Nobody knew why.

Maybe Dan Slattery had some idea why Cane ran for the train. Dan kept mum during the next week. He took to shaking his head, as if he were saying "no" to himself. He stood at a spot behind the old bar where he could see down Depot Street, in front of Little Egypt. He watched, but he didn't say what for. He watched all week. Nothing he was watching for came.

"Who you expecting, Slattery?" Jake said to him, when he was feeling high. "You watching for Russell? Or Cane? Or who?"

"Shut up," said Slattery. He kept on watching. When he

thought Jake was looking the other way, he shook his head to himself.

* * *

Brice had been made executor of Mr. Trimble's estate; and it took him a long time to clear up some of Trimble's affairs. He spent a day, almost every week, going through receipts and vouchers and notes in the library at Trimble's dark old house, though he didn't like being there. Brice was used to dead bodies, but not to houses that seemed as if they were going to start talking any minute. Nearly a month after the fire at Little Egypt, Brice came puffing up the street toward Russell's office and saw Jake going the other way and told him to come along; there might be a job for him.

They hurried into Russell's place, Jake not knowing what it was all about; and Deputy Russell, seeing Brice's face, said, "Something special?"

"I found something in a Bible at the Trimble house," Brice told him, pulling a scrap of paper out of his vest pocket.

Russell took the paper, but didn't unfold it for a minute. "Didn't know you were a Bible reader, Brice," said Russell, who was one.

"It wasn't me that took the Bible off the shelf." Brice said it as if someone were going to call him a liar. "Somebody put it in the middle of Trimble's desk, open. I never touched a book in that house."

"Anybody been there since you left last week?" Russell asked him. Not that he knew of, said Brice. Russell and Brice looked at each other a second. "Just where was this paper stuck?" said Russell.

"What made you ask that?" Brice said. "It's a funny thing. I wrote down the book, chapter, and verse: Ezekiel, eighth chapter, eighth verse, at the top of the page. Look it up."

Russell took his own Bible from the whatnot in the corner, and read aloud to Brice and Jake:

> "Now will I shortly pour out my fury upon thee and accomplish mine anger upon thee; and I will judge thee according to thy ways, and will recompense thee for all thy abominations."

"Let's see that paper," was all Jake had to say. Russell unfolded it. It didn't look as if it had been in a Bible for a while; it looked fresh, hardly creased. Russell said as much to Brice.

"I hope to die if that isn't where I found it," Brice told them. "I know what it says, but read it."

Russell did: "Jingo on the stove. Two men, backs turned; another at door. McCunn's cutter."

"Whose writing?" asked Brice.

"Trimble's, looks like," said Russell. "Let's move. I'm going over to talk with Larry McCunn. You two get hold of some men and drift around Little Egypt. Watch the doors."

Russell drove off, whipping up his horse, toward McCunn's; Jake was game for trouble, and he rounded up two other fellows, and with Brice they went toward Little Egypt.

Larry McCunn was a washed-out sort, scared of his shadow, and Russell didn't have to talk to him long. On the day Jingo Criminy died, McCunn's cousin Red Fellows had borrowed McCunn's horse and cutter. Fellows and Cane and Slattery weren't the boys McCunn could say no to, or the boys he could blab about afterward. McCunn told Russell all he knew, and then Russell let him go and rode for Little Egypt.

The saloon still was smoked up from the fire, and the door was sagging, and Russell never saw a fouler, tougher place. There wasn't a soul inside but Fellows, half asleep. Russell was glad of that. He sat down opposite Fellows and asked where Bloody Dan was. "At the butcher shop, I guess," Fellows told him.

"Then maybe you won't hang, Red," said Russell. "McCunn had a talk with me. There's you and Slattery. Slattery's enough to hang."

Fellows gave in; something had been eating him since Cane ran away. He whined like an old hound. "It was Dan planned it. Dan finished Jingo that way. It was Dan that got behind Trimble." He talked on, while Russell nodded. Then, of a sudden, Russell knew somebody else was in the saloon, and he looked over Fellows' shoulder. The backroom door stood open; Bloody Dan had come in; he had his meat ax in his hand.

Russell knocked over his chair and ran for the door. Fellows twisted round, and squealed, and got up, but not soon enough. Slattery split him.

Russell went down the front steps like water over a dam. Jake and Brice picked him up, and the other men bunched together, watching the doorway. "For God's sake," Russell called to the men in back of the tavern, "don't let Dan slip out that way." A crowd was outside now—women and boys, and half the men in town. "Well," said Russell, "we better go after him, if we don't want him coming out on us."

People looked at Jake, who was swinging a blacksmith's hammer. "Come on," said Jake, and went up the steps.

Fellows was in front of the bar, and his head was in two pieces. "I thought Dan used that ax on Mr. Trimble," was what Jake said. Dan? Nowhere. Not in the backroom or the kitchen. Four men with guns went through the rooms upstairs, peeking round corners; but they turned out only Baldy and little Sam. Everybody had his mind on that meat ax: Little Egypt was dark and Dan was fast.

"It'll be the cellar," said Jake. They gathered around the trap in the backroom floor. "Sure as hell he's down there." Nobody spoke above a whisper.

"I think there's a little window to the cellar on the north side," Russell said. "I'll see if I can get through that way. Anybody willing to try the trap at the same time?" He and Brice looked at Jake, who spat and shifted to his other foot.

"Dan's got the ax and maybe a gun," Jake told them. "Burn the skunk out." He reached for the oven door.

"No, it ain't lawful," Russell said. "We got to go after him."

"All right," said Jake. "But break the glass in that window the minute you see my legs on the ladder. And close the trap behind me, boys; I don't want Dan sighting on me."

Russell ran out. They opened the cellar door; Jake waited a bit, and then heard a pane break, and scooted down the ladder into the dark. And as he went down, and as the trap closed above him, everyone heard a screech: a screech that shook the floor and froze every man and made Jake slip when halfway down the ladder and fall to the dirt at the bottom.

"Not Slattery, if I know Slattery," Brice said, up in the backroom. They had left the trap just a bit ajar, so that Jake could have a glint of light.

Jake huddled at the bottom, looking out for Dan's ax, and for whatever had screeched. It was an old stone cellar, full of cobwebs and broken bottles. Jake could see no one; but as his eyes became used to the darkness, he made out an open hole in the corner, probably a dry cistern, and not very deep. Had they put what was left of Trimble there, before they drove the surrey to the crossing? Jake crawled to the edge, expecting to feel that ax any second.

There they were: one man flat on the cistern bottom, looking as if he'd been broken in the middle, and the other tugging at him, so as to lift the body the five or six feet to the lip of the cistern. Dan was the smashed man; his ax was away at the far side of the hole. Jake took a real breath for the first time since he'd gone through the trap. "That's a good job, Russell," Jake said. "Shove Dan up, and I'll pull."

Now the man down in the dark below had Slattery's big body over his shoulders. He straightened slowly, and brought the dead man almost level with Jake's face. Dan's head flopped on one side: the neck was broken. Jake caught hold of the shoulders and began to pull. Just then, Russell said, "Jake, are you there? Is that you? I can't get through the damned window."

For a quarter of a second, Jake looked round to where Russell's voice came from. Yes, Russell was looking through the little window; he still was outside the cellar, too fat to crawl through. Jake snapped his head back toward the cistern as quick as an owl. The man in the hole was shoving Slattery's body toward him, and as he rose under the weight, he and Jake came face to face, a foot or two apart. The man in the cistern had a black beard; and he had green eyes; and he had a little puckering scar running up from one eyelid. Jake saw this, and he sucked in his breath, and let go Dan's body; and it fell back into the cistern. Then Jake was at the foot of the ladder, and up in two jumps, and into the backroom.

Jake broke the neck off a bottle of whiskey, and poured it down himself, but no one could get a word out of him except "Trimble, Trimble, Trimble." Brice and two other men went down the ladder; they found Dan dead with a broken neck and a broken back in the little cistern, and nothing else. Russell still was at the window, pointing a shotgun through: all he had seen was Jake, or somebody he took to be Jake, kneeling by the cistern and then diving for the ladder.

That's all. What do you expect me to tell you? Jake never drank again. No one lived in Trimble's house afterward, for his mark was on it. It's been twenty years since it burned. All the rest of his life Jake watched, the way Slattery watched for a week or two; but nothing ever came to him. They're all in the graveyard now, Uncle Jake and the lot, and before you know it, I'll be with them. And because I never had powers like Amos Trimble's, I'll lie easy there.

SKYBERIA

⌂

On that cold autumn day—the sun hidden since early morning—two men were lost in Skyberia. Whatever new ragged ridge they sighted resembled every other; each conical sinkhole they struggled through seemed familiar yet menacingly unique. Their compass could not help them, for Clements and Robertson did not know what direction they ought to take; now and then the sky emitted a contemptuous sprinkle of snow, otherwise preserving its gray mask of a celestial caducity; and though several times they fired their rifles, they heard no other report in all those illimitable second-growth woods. Even the deer they were hunting never broke cover, so that Clements and Robertson told each other they were fools for leaving the pit-blind they had dug, to look for deer instead of shivering in their hole.

As afternoon wore on, they heard a dog howling, howling far away through the jack pines and tamaracks and cedars.

Skyberia, which has no precise frontiers, is a resurrected forest, in part the domain of the state by virtue of delinquent tax confiscations, in part a patchwork of abandoned or moribund farms over which the scrub creeps slowly back. A wood that has inched back from its grave has the look of Lazarus upon it. Clements and Robertson, who knew nothing of wild country, thought a beeline the quickest route and therefore repeatedly left the ridges and fought across the sinkholes, sometimes slipping ankle-deep in ooze and getting thoroughly scared.

And the sky watched them from behind the gray and drooped lids of its eyes. Blue or gray or black, the sky watched whatever living things ventured into Skyberia. Smokeless and empty, forever popping unexpectedly from behind a pine-veiled ridge, the sky lords it over Skyberia: in few other corners of the world is the sky so tyrannical. An ironic old man in Bear City, who knew these woods as well as anyone did, had clapped the "Skyberia" to them, and the name stuck. Under this sneeringly vigilant sky, Clements and Robertson stood bewildered, listening to the distant dog howl.

Clements sold cars in Cleveland; Robertson held a sinecure in the highway department. Either, in his secret heart, would have preferred watching football over his television set to this wet and chill plodding through shadow-land. Yet a compulsion to show their manliness impelled them every autumn into the northern woods, where the bucks as regularly eluded them. They wore high-laced engineers' boots, exhausting for long tramps; their shoulders ached under the weight of their mackinaws; they would have liked to throw their guns into the swamp. The dog howled on; and after conferring, Clements and Robertson resumed their beeline course toward the howl. For all the cold, they were sweating when they found the dog.

An oasis in Skyberia, fifteen or twenty cleared acres, formed a gulf in the woods. Down to the far side of this pasture ran a mud track, and rusty barbed wire, strung eccentrically to uprooted stumps, had kept the deer out more or less, and the cattle in. But now there was no need for a fence. The tar-paper shanty which stood on the northern edge of the field was deserted, they could see—the door open, the chimney smokeless. A privy and a shed and the wreck of a chicken coop—these were all the buildings of this Skyberian farm. Big and black, half collie, half Newfoundland, the dog sat beside the door and howled, his head averted from Clements and Robertson.

"What's he up to?" asked Robertson, edgily.

"Towse doesn't forget in a hurry." A slow, rather nasal voice said this, out of nowhere, and Clements and Robertson faced about with a common apprehension. In the shadow of the chicken-house a man was standing, one foot on an old crate; he must have been watching them as they approached the clearing. Tall, lean, somewhat stooped, he inspected them out of large brown eyes. His hair, showing beneath a cap with ear flaps, was bushy and reddish; deep lines, set in a whimsical expression, ran sharply down this tanned face on either side of his mouth; he wore an old field-jacket and blue denims. Seeing him apparently amiable, Clements and Robertson had hopes of getting back that night to their tourist cabin outside Bear City.

"Say!" Clements began. "This your place, friend? I hope we're not trespassing. We didn't see any signs up."

"No, not mine." The tall man—somewhere about fifty years old, perhaps—came into the deserted yard. "This was the Hallecks' house, but a couple of weeks ago they finally stopped trying to scratch a living. They gave Towse to me then, but every other day or so he trots back here, and I have to fetch him. It's a cold sight, eh? The door swings open, the squirrels go in and out of the window, and the black dog is master of all he surveys."

Clements and Robertson regarded the tall man uneasily. "Does that come from Kipling?" asked Robertson, meaning to be polite.

"It comes from Williams, so far as I know," the tall man answered him placidly. "Samuel Williams is my name. Tom!" He shouted toward the woods beyond the faint trail; a small boy came loping. "That's my son, Tom." Williams glanced wryly at their boots. "Been out a good many hours?"

"Ever since nine," Clements said fervently. "We've rented a cabin close to town. Left our car on the other side of the ridges."

"You could stand some coffee. Come along, and after we stop at my place, I'll take you back to your car, or close to it." Williams grasped the reluctant Towse by the scruff of the neck and set out along the vestige of a road, Tom silent beside him; Clements and Robertson, aching at every joint, tried to match his stride.

Samuel Williams seemed content to be silent. Clements, uneasy in the stillness of the vanishing road, dimly longing for the noise of traffic and the reek of gasoline and the demanding bumble of voices that made the stuff of his normal existence, wanted very much to talk. But though volubility was his vocation, for almost the first time in his life he was uncertain how to commence. Whatever did people back in these sticks talk about? They probably would not have television sets, so television programs were out; the fact that for a long time, obviously, no motor-car had forced its way along this trail somehow discouraged mention of an interest almost universal: the new car models; and he rather doubted whether this weather-ravaged man kept up with college football. So Clements reverted, without preliminaries, to the subject really at the back of his mind, and asked: "What do you folks do in these parts, Mr. Williams?"

As though uncertain of what was meant by the question, Williams hesitated. "You mean how we get along? It's a bit of this and a bit of that. A few acres of corn, some potatoes and beans and cucumbers, half a dozen steers run in the woods and grained in the winter, a couple of cows, the chickens—there's most of it. Apple trees and peaches, too. Plenty of blackberries and huckleberries in the woods, fish enough in the lakes, and a little venison one time or another." Here he seemed inclined to wink, but thought better of it. "The elevator in town takes the beans and pickles— that accounts for most of the cash. And I can turn a hand to a job of carpentry or brick-laying, if somebody round about needs a house or a barn built. We need more cash than my father and his folks did, of course. They made their clothes and they never bought canned goods; they were close people, but they never borrowed. They lived in a farmer's world, Mister, and we live in a city man's world. How about you?"

Robertson explained who they were; Williams only nodded. Towse, obedient now, trotted ahead; Tom surreptitiously inspected the two strangers with the extreme shyness of old-fashioned children, a juvenile phenomenon unfamiliar and disturbing to Clements and Robertson. A rabbit, hardly shyer, dodged across the track.

"Have you any other kids, Mr. Williams?" asked Robertson, loudly, as if he were in a noisy office. "Williams!" sighed an echo from the ridge which the road now paralleled. Clements jumped; he did not like Nature, really, he confessed to himself.

"Three others, a good deal older than Tom," Williams answered. "Rachel's the nearest; she got married and went to Chicago. The girls mostly go, because they see the movies and then can't stand to be sand-hill savages like me. They think happiness is a gear in a machine—all you have to do is shift and you'll be happy. And there's Andrew. He's a machinist at Oldsmobile, and comes home once or twice a year. They get better than two-fifty an hour, in his department, which seems pretty nice to them. But after rent and income tax and Social Security and payments on his car and what it takes to eat in the city, what does Andrew get that his dad doesn't? Yet they don't see this; they'll live in the smoke and the noise and the mess of last Sunday's papers and with a couple of babies in a pre-fab, as long as wages hold out. They don't see it. They tell me that with a city job, you don't have to face the weather and you don't have to put up with a lonely winter." Here Williams fell silent.

"Did you say there were four, altogether?" Clements put in.

"With Ed, yes," Williams told him. "Probably Ed would

have stuck; he had grit; but south of Florence a land mine took off both his legs. They don't come back whole, not the farmers and the farmers' sons. They're the fellows that need arms and legs most, but they don't bring them back from the war with them. Because they're used to rough life and to handling guns, the army puts them in the infantry right off. Some don't come back whole; some just don't come back. You'd think, from the casualty rate, that the people who run the cities decided that whatever country boys they didn't seem able to tempt off the farm or starve out, they'd bury. Ed might have stuck. Well, Tom's got some spunk in him: he may stay out of the factory." He gave the boy a nod, and Tom retreated behind the big dog. "And here's my place now, gentlemen."

This gap in Skyberia was appreciably larger than the desolate Halleck farm; and the house was no shanty, but a long, tight cabin of squared lobs, neat though old, with kitchen and woodshed tacked solidly to the rear of it. As they approached, a stout woman came out of the door, with some hesitation, straightening her apron. "My wife Alice," said Williams, introducing Clements and Robertson. She seemed good-humored at this apparition of guests, promised a bit of supper, and withdrew into the kitchen. Clements and Robertson took chairs by the black iron stove and eyed the room while they talked with Williams. The interior surface of the logs was plastered, so that the cabin was warm; but it was very simple. Worn blue linoleum on the floor, three or four straight chairs, a sofa with slip covers, an old easy chair, a plain square table, a desk, a china cabinet, and a top-heavy bookcase—this was nearly all the furniture. Curtains made of dyed army blankets hung in two small doorways, the entrances to bedrooms. No radio, no electric light—for a big kerosene lamp stood on the table—probably no running water.

"You've a cozy little place here," Clements remarked, hypocritically. "Wish I had one like it to spend the summers in."

"Oh, it's a comfortable house for these parts. My father made half the furniture. We keep warm, because there's plenty of time in winter for sawing wood. When the snow's deep, there's no getting to town, but Alice does a lot of fall canning and we stay here snug enough until the snow-plough from the county barns comes around, or there's a thaw."

"But you must be bored stiff," Robertson objected with a kind of horror, thinking of endless winter nights without company, without bridge or canasta, without television or movies, without liquor or change of scene or the slightest alteration. He thought of the white woods all round, the sigh of the wind, the incessant, intolerable quiet.

A slow smile spread across Williams' gaunt face. "Why, I look forward to the winters. The chores don't let up, but still a good deal of time's left over. Alice and Tom and I sit in the kitchen and talk, or maybe I stretch out on the sofa with one of those." He pointed a thumb toward the massive oak bookcase. "Some were Dad's, and some were Ed's—Ed was a deep boy, and quick besides—and some I picked up. I hear nobody reads down your way, these days; too busy, too much television."

"Last Christmas I tackled *The Big Fisherman*," Clements said, hoping to be agreeable. "But when you're in business . . ." He moved to the bookcase. "Say, this is serious stuff: *Rise of the Dutch Republic*, by Motley; *The Virginians*, by William Makepeace Thackeray; *Ayesha*, by Rider Haggard; *Essays*, by Emerson; *Plutarch's Lives*. And you've got a big Bible here. You read all these books?"

"Most. I'm a slow reader, though. What's the hurry? If I kept at it till doomsday, I'd never be half as smart as Ed. Some of Ed's books are hard sledding for an old hand like me, but now and then I feel as if I ought to have a look at them because Ed can't. I've taken to reading the Bible, too, after all these years. Ordinarily it's too long a trip to town to make church on Sunday, and the church at New Salem Corners that was closer, burned three years ago. Anyway, there hadn't been a regular minister for ten years before, because there weren't enough of us left around here to pay one. But I've been reading the Bible out loud to Alice and Tom some time now. Don't get nervous, friends: I'm not one of those 'Jesus Saves' folks, asking you about the state of your souls. Yet in the past three or four years, I've begun to understand why God is terrible. You and I and everybody else know, deep down, that our world is going to smash. And I'm thinking that God wants it to smash. He wants it to smash because He's terrible. And He's terrible because he loves us."

Clements and Robertson were experiencing that profound embarrassment which engulfs moderns trapped into hearing a confession of faith. "I go to the First Baptist quite often . . ." said Robertson, feebly defensive.

"He's terrible," Williams went on, "because He wants us to be human. He loves us because we're human. But we've been trying to make ourselves inhuman, and that's why He intends to let this age smash. He's going to make us resume being human again. The cities . . ."

Here, however, Mrs. Williams brought in the supper, and her husband pulled up chairs for Clements and Robertson. It was clear that the Williamses seldom had company, for there were not enough cups to go round: Tom and Mrs. Williams drank their coffee out of bowls. "Hey, bluegills!" Robertson exclaimed cordially. A big platter of fish, and a dish of baked potatoes, and homemade bread, and home-canned peaches—this was their meal, everything decently cooked. Clements and Robertson did justice to it. Temporarily, indeed, the food made them almost at ease in Skyberia; they even could imagine themselves living on bluegills in the woods indefinitely.

"I don't see why you don't have more neighbors," said Clements, helping himself to more peaches, "seeing you live so well. Anyone moved away recently besides the Hallecks?"

"A dozen years ago," Mrs. Williams answered him, "there were eight or ten families through here. Now we're the last. The church is gone, the school's gone, the store's gone. In the whole township there are just seventeen registered voters, and fewer still in the next township. And the more that go away, the harder it is for those that stay."

Robertson said he could not understand why. "I thought the government was helping you farmers."

Williams' sardonic grin stopped him. "You're thinking of the big fellows, the wheat men and the cotton men and the cattle men. Not us fellows, not us fools who eat what we raise. They pay the big fellows by taking the difference out of our hides. It's the same way with most everything. They closed down our little school before Tom was old enough to attend, and told us we'd have to send our kids to the consolidated school at Bear City—the bus would come for them. But if you have to send your children half across the county to a school you've no say in—why, you might as well live in the city, eh? Anyhow, that's what some folks thought, and they're in the city now. And the people that run the cities are thinking up ways of dealing with stubborn codgers like yours truly.

"Well, if you want to get to your cabin tonight, I suppose we'd best get on the road."

While Clements and Robertson pulled on their coats beside the stove, Williams and his boy got out their team and wagon. Mrs. Williams brought blankets to wrap round their legs. "We used to have a Model T," she apologized, "but even it began to wear out, and parts got harder to find, and the new cars don't get many miles to the gallon. Sam says that's a good sign: the factories are slipping. So we stick to the wagon and do well enough, but I hope you can stand the cold."

With effusive thanks, they said goodbye to her, and then Williams, Tom on the seat beside him, shook the reins; and they bumped down the dim track, the dark of the forest oppressive upon them, for it now was long past sundown. After nearly an hour's tiring ride, they began to enter country which, despite the darkness, seemed less unfamiliar to Clements and Robertson. "We'll find that car of yours any minute now," Williams declared.

"How long are you going to stick it out in these woods, Mr. Williams?" Clements asked.

"Well, sir," Williams said, "I know now that I'm going

to stand it as long as I live; and so is Tom, probably. Five years ago—yes, two or three years ago—I wouldn't have given a plugged nickel for our chances of holding out. But you remember what I said about God's being terrible. Not long past I was certain, sure as Hell's a mantrap, that the game was up for little fellows like me. The Government, the unions, the chain stores, the consolidated schools, the factories, the Army, the movies, radio, television, and Old Man Arithmetic had our number. But now I think I was wrong: because God is terrible, and He loves men, and He's going to make them keep their human nature. He's not intending to let us copy ants. He's not going to turn us over to the social workers and the planners and the generals and the organizers. He's going to burn us, and He's going to starve us, but He'll keep us men. No, Tom and I will be here when nearly everything else has flamed to blue blazes."

Now some big dark object blocked the road: Williams swung his lantern toward it, and it turned into Clements' Buick. Clements and Robertson scrambled awkwardly down from the wagon, shuffled their feet in the half-inch of snow, thanked Williams again, offered him a five-dollar bill which he would not take, and presently warmed up the Buick. While the motor idled, Williams stood by the car door; and Robertson asked him, abruptly, with a nervous laugh, "What'll you sell your place for?"

"I'll never sell, by the Almighty," Williams pronounced. "Time was when I'd have sold for a thousand dollars; time was when I'd have sold for five hundred dollars, and have been thankful. Why, I believe there was a time when, if you'd offered me a steady job in town, I'd have given you the place. But not now, nor ever again. I thank God He put me in Skyberia. There's a time at hand when people in the cities will look for rats and cats to eat, and there'll be none. Or if they don't starve, or burn, then the city people will be like soft machines that have to be fed and watched and replaced; they won't be *men*; they'll be things that take and take, but never give. Things like that don't endure long. But Skyberia will be here when the rest of the world has eaten itself up; and we'll be people here in Skyberia, not ants or rabbits."

"What about guys like Robertson here, and me, when blue blazes come?" Clements inquired, trying to smile.

Removing his cap, Williams tucked it in his belt, drew off his right glove, and shook hands with Clements and Robertson. "Goodbye, gentlemen." He said this and nothing more; and as the Buick rolled toward Bear City, he stood silent in the cold, watching them vanish into the world of progress that lies beyond Skyberia.

Presently Williams put his cap on, climbed to the wagon seat beside little Tom, and urged his team back along the road. They had gone hardly two hundred yards when the lantern light flashed upon some scrap of metal lying between the ruts—a chunk of iron, fallen from a truck or farm machine. Samuel Williams reined in the horses. "Jump down, Tom," he said, gently, "and get us that thing. From now on, we'll need to save scraps." This done, they made again for home, the snow and stumps and second growth of Skyberia closing behind them like the doors of Ali Baba's cavern.

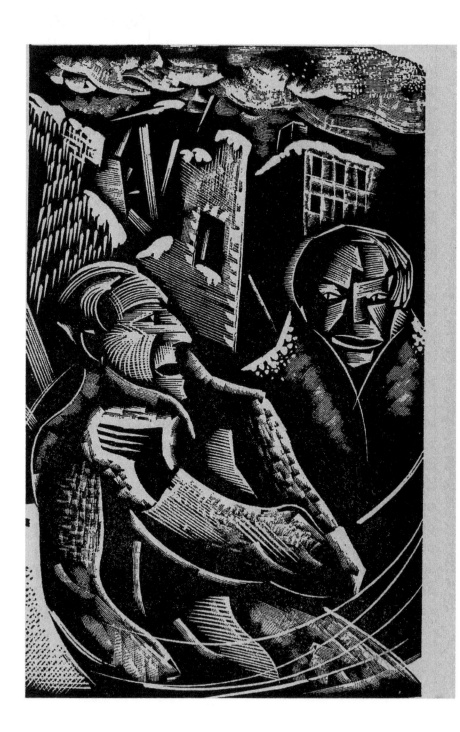

SORWORTH PLACE

◊

> "But the age of chivalry is gone. . . . The unbought grace of life, the cheap defence of nations, the nurse of manly sentiment and heroic enterprise is gone. It is gone, that sensibility of principle, that chastity of honor, which felt a stain like a wound, which inspired courage whilst it mitigated ferocity, which ennobled whatever it touched, and under which vice itself lost half its evil, by losing all its grossness."
> —Edmund Burke, *Reflections on the Revolution in France*

In defiance of a faint ancient charm that perfumes its name, Sorworth today is a dirty and dreary little town, fouled by the colliery since the pit was sunk and a blot of hideous industrial workers' houses began to spread about it. The lanes are half derelict, now that the pit approaches exhaustion. At a turn of the High Street, or down close off the Back Vennel, some fragments of old Scots masonry stand yet amidst a welter of hoardings and "fish restaurants" and corrugated iron roofing.

To damp Sorworth, of all places, Mr. Ralph Bain, M.C., had contrived to drift at the end of a month of purposeless nights in "family and commercial" hotels or bare village taverns across three counties. Drinks with strangers in one village, listless games of cards in the next town, inconsequential talks on buses or trains, dull glimpses of a pleasant wood there, an old church here: thus February had run out, and the next little pension check would be forwarded to him at Sorworth, which spot he had chosen at random as his address for the first few days of March.

Bain lounged by the door of the "King's Arms" in his old tweeds (with the cigarette-burns neatly darned) and felt the crack in his skull more vexatious than usual, and shifted his long legs languidly. Sorworth had nothing to show him. But what place had? He lit a cigarette, though he already had smoked three more this morning than he once resolved to allow himself out of the indispensable pension check.

At that moment, a girl came out of a provision shop across the square, walking obliquely past the market-cross in the direction of the "King's Arms"; and Bain, one hand cupped to shelter his match, his face inclined slightly downward, noticed the remarkable grace of her little feet. He glanced lazily up; then he threw away his match, let his cigarette go unlit, and instinctively straightened. He had not seen this lady before, but in that second it passed through his mind, whimsically, "Perhaps she's what drew me to Sorworth."

Surely a man might travel a great way without meeting such a face as hers—pale, very pale, with lips a glowing natural red, and black hair gathered with taste at the back of her head into a heavy roll that rested upon her firm shoulders. Her chin, too, was delicately firm. She carried herself with a dignity that seems to be dying from modern life, looking straight ahead, as if in some reverie that walled her away from the grossness of Sorworth—yet not (Bain judged from her mouth) a reverie wholly pleasant. Among the mill girls and shop-assistants and bedraggled housewives in Sorworth, there was none anything like her; and few anywhere else. As she passed by the "King's Arms," she seemed to notice Bain; their eyes met, briefly; then she lowered her lashes, unsmiling, and was gone up the Vennel.

"Och, she's a bonnie one, Mrs. Lurlin." Happening to come to the door as the girl passed by, old MacLeod, who kept the "King's Arms," had followed Bain's long look. "There wullna be her like for aye, Mr. Bain—not at auld Sorworth Place." MacLeod shook his head portentously. In his youth he had been a gardener at some house of Lord Bute's, and he continued to hold the county families in profound respect, muttering sourly about Communists among the miners who drank in his bar.

"She's young to have the care of a big house," said Bain, relapsed into lethargy, and lighting his cigarette at last.

"Aye, and wee tae be widowed, sir. Noo the hoose—she canna hope tae keep it in the auld way, ye ken. Twa maids, and they carlines fu' o' girnings, sir: sma' comfort in a cauld hoose that na sae canny, when a's said. It will be rack and ruin, forbye, wi' half the grand hooses in the county." And MacLeod proceeded to expatiate on his favorite topics, the decay of old families and the follies of socialism.

"A widow?" put in Bain, lifting his heavy eyelids a bit. "She couldn't have been married a great while. What was this Lurlin like?"

"Be wha' he was, sir, the gentleman's dead, dead the year noo, Mr. Bain; and sma' gude claverin' o' men in the grave." That said, MacLeod turned back into his pub; but Bain, surprised at this reticence in a publican who ordinarily manifested a full share of Scottish censoriousness, followed him.

"He didn't die in the war?" inquired Bain.

"Na, na," said MacLeod, thus brought to bay; and, presently, "The drink, sir, the drink; that, and mair. Dinna mistake me, Mr. Bain. The Lurlins were braw auld blude; aye, but this Mr. Alastair Lurlin, he wasna o' the proper line, ye ken—na mair than a cousin. Mr. Hamish Lurlin, the auld laird, died seven years syne, and his twa sons were shot in Libya, first Alexander, then Hew. A' three death duties maun be paid, and the cousin comes tae wha's left. Last year, this Mr. Alastair dies: mair duties. Weel, Mrs. Lurlin keeps the hoose, and the policies, and a bit moor besides. Ninety thousand acres Lurlin o' Sorworth had, before the first war. Noo, but a hoose wha's unco cauld and clammy. Come awa' upstairs, sir, if ye be sae fascinated"—this a trifle spitefully—"and ye can see the auld Place frae the attic, if ye ha' gude een."

From a garret window of the "King's Arms," they looked over the pantiles and corrugated iron roofs of the shabby town toward a serrated ridge some miles westward. On a flank of that hill, Bain just could make out the grey shape of a big ancient house, wraithlike against the heather and gorse and bracken. "There'll be nane aulder in the county," said MacLeod.

Bain went down alone to the parlor, sat some minutes before the doddering fire, and then addressed a note to Mrs. Lurlin, Sorworth Place. He was, he wrote truthfully enough, rather a dilettante in architecture; recently he had heard her house spoken of as remarkable; he would be glad to see it, if no inconvenience would be caused; and he would be in Sorworth the rest of the week. After some hesitation, he signed himself "M. C.": the Military Cross, after all, was one of his few remaining links with decent society, and he had the right to use it.

This letter posted, he went up to his room, brushed his old tweed suit, and glanced at himself in the mirror: the heavy eyes, the long and regular features weakened by lines of indecision, the defiant half-grin of bravado. He grimaced, and the suture in the back of his head—a memento of the shell fragment that had given him his pension—winced in sympathy. To escape from self-dislike, he went down to the bar, very like fleeing from the cell into the jailyard.

* * *

Late the next afternoon an answer to his note came, written in a small round hand, which said that Mr. Bain would be shown about Sorworth Place if he should call on Thursday afternoon, and was signed "Ann Lurlin." The firm signature put Bain in mind of Mrs. Lurlin's elegant, pale look; and he spent most of the intervening evening and night and morning in a reverie of nearly forgotten faces, men he had alienated by his negligence or his improvidence, women he had found hollow or who had found him exasperating. None of these ever thought of him now, even when dreaming before the fire. And why should they?

Shortly past noon on Thursday, he walked along an empty road toward the ridge called Sorworth Law; the road became a lane between high and crumbling stone dykes; and then he was at the entrance to a neglected park on the side of a hill, its gates vanished, its gatelodge empty, all its larger trees felled by some timber merchant and the stumps left among heaps of dead leaves. Bain turned up the drive, and soon he could see, on the bare slope above, the massive stone shape of the Place of Sorworth.

Two square towers, at either end; and between them, extending also far to the rear, an immense block of building, in part ashlar, but mostly rubble. None of this, except a fine large window above the entrance, was later than the seventeenth century, and most was far older. An intricacy of crowstepped gables, turrets, dormers, and chimneys confused one's eyes when they roved upward. All in all, the Place was an admirable example of the Scots mansion house unprettified by Balmoralism. A flight of heavy stone steps led up to the door, and on either side of the entrance projected a conical-capped turret, each supported at its base by an enormous corbel, curiously bevelled.

Some rods to the north could be made out to be what was left of a detached building, the roof of it gone—a chapel, perhaps. So far as Bain could see, there were only two entrances: the grand portal, and a small heavy door with a wrought-iron grill before it, that probably gave upon the kitchen. At the angles of either tower, musket-holes or arrow-loops, some blocked with mortar, the rest now closed with small panes of glass, flanked the entrance. The roofs were of ancient stone slabs.

Away at the back, the stout dykes of a walled garden closed the view, although Bain could hear the rushing of a burn somewhere in that direction. The lawn before the Place was unkempt, no better than pasture; and there, in one of the towers and even in the main block, a broken pane glinted in the afternoon sun, and all about the strong grey house hung a suggestion of neglect and impoverishment that would have been more clearly manifest, doubtless, had not the mansion been so severe and rugged in its very character. The huge window of what must be the great hall broke the solidity of the façade just above the main door. Between this window and the doorway below, Bain perceived, as he climbed the steps, a terribly weathered coat of arms executed in a soft red sandstone, appended to it some pious inscription in venerably barbarous Scots-Latin characters, most of them indecipherable. He could read only the two words which composed the last line: L-A-R-V-A R-E-S-U-R-G-A-T. *Larva Resurgat?* Why *larva*, rather than *spiritus?* The old lairds sometimes put things quaintly. He found no bell and so banged at the oaken door with a rusty knocker.

After an interval of leaden silence, the door was pulled ajar a bit, and a sour woman's face peeked round it. Bain asked to be announced. The fat maid let him into a little round room with naked stone walls, at the stairfoot, and locked the door again and then conducted him up a twisting stone stair in one of the entrance turrets—its treads scooped hollow by centuries of feet—to a gigantic vaulted chamber, well lighted: the hall. It was fitted with sixteenth-century panelling, painted with heraldic symbols and family crests. The air was cold, the yawning medieval fireplace quite empty; here and there a Jacobean carved cupboard, or the polished surface of a table, or a tapestried chair endeavored to apologize for the emptiness of the Place. None of the furniture seemed in good repair. Bain sat gingerly on a Chippendale piece, while the maid scurried off to some hidie-hole in this labyrinth of a house.

After three or four minutes, Mrs. Lurlin came down to him, emerging from behind a door concealed by a hanging.

A faint smile hovered on her fine lips, her eyes met his composedly, and Bain thought her most beautiful, in an antique fashion. "I'll show you the curiosities of this draughty place, Mr. Bain," she said, in a low voice with an agreeable suggestion of west coast accent about it, "if you'll pledge yourself to ignore dust and damp. I've nothing left but the house and the policies and a bit of moor, you know—not even a home farm."

Bain hardly knew what he said in reply, for she unsettled him, as if he had been shaken awake. Then Mrs. Lurlin led him up disused stairs and down into vaulted cellars and through chambers with mouldering tapestries and Lord knows where else. Almost all these interminable rooms were empty.

"Most was gone before the place became mine," said Mrs. Lurlin, without visible embarrassment, "but I had to sell what was left of the furniture, except for a few sticks in the really necessary rooms. I suppose the wreckers will buy the house when I'm dead. You can sell an eighteenth-century house, just possibly, in spite of rates, but not a behemoth like this. I can't afford to live here; but I can't afford to go away, either. Do you have some great barn of this sort, Mr. Bain?"

"I haven't even a cottage," Bain told her, "or a stick of furniture." He thought her black eyes remarkably candid.

She took him up to the summit of one of the towers, where they stood in the wind and looked over the braes that parallel the den of Sorworth Water as it twists down to the sharp-toothed long skerries where it meets the sea. From this height they could see quite clearly the surf on the rocks, and, some distance south, smoke from the fishing village of Sorworthness. Sorworth Water was in spate. Just at the tower's foot, the den veered right up to the castle, so that a stone which Bain tossed over the rampart bounced down a steep slope into the roaring burn. In the rough old days, the lairds of Sorworth had the security of a strongly situated house. "You're not afraid of heights, Mr. Bain?" asked this young woman.

"No," he said, "I've climbed a good deal."

"I fancy you're afraid of very little," she observed, lifting her eyebrows slightly. "Do you know that I happened to see you in the square two days ago? I thought you looked like a soldier. What were you?"

He had been a captain, he told her.

"Come down into the policies, Captain Bain," she said. As they descended, he bumped his head against a window ledge, and cried out involuntarily. She stopped, with an exclamation of sympathy.

"A mortar put a crack in my skull," Bain apologized, "and I'm still tender, and probably always will be."

"Does it pain you much, Captain Bain?"

"No; but perhaps I ought to tell you that it makes me a trifle odd, now and then. Or so people seem to think." He did not mind confiding this to her: perhaps it was the oddity he had just acknowledged, but at the moment they two seemed to him the only realities in an infinity of shadows.

"So much the better," she said, still lower—either that or something of the sort.

"I beg your pardon, Mrs. Lurlin?"

"I mean this, Captain Bain: we seem to be birds of a feather. People hereabouts think I am rather odd. Sorworth

Place is soaked in oddity. The maids won't stay. I've only one, now; the other went last week, and even Margaret, who's left, won't sleep in—she goes down to her son's cottage. I don't suppose you know why Janet went, unless someone at the "King's Arms" told you the gossip. Well, Janet wouldn't stay because she thought something whispered to her in the cellars. Poor timid creature! It was all fancy; for if anything were to whisper, you know, it would whisper to *me*. Would you like to see the garden? Most of it has gone back, of course."

They poked about the overgrown walks of the policies, talking of trifles, and presently strayed near the chapel ruin. "May I glance inside?" asked Bain.

"There's very little . . ." she answered, somewhat sharply. But Bain already had passed through the broken doorway. Some defaced sixteenth- and seventeenth-century monuments were fixed to the walls, and a litter of leaves encumbered the pavement. Where his feet scattered these, Bain noticed two or three ancient bronze rings fixed in stone slabs; and, being rather vain of his strength of arm, he bent, gripped one of them, and pulled upward. The stone lifted very slightly, though it was heavy, and when Bain let go the ring, the slab settled back with a dull reverberation.

"O, for God's sake, stop!"

He swung round to her. That delicate pallor of her young face had gone grey; she clutched at the door moulding for support. Bain took her hands in his, to save her from falling, and led her toward the house. "What is it, Mrs. Lurlin?" He felt mingled alarm and pleasure thus to have a bond between them—even the terror in her eyes.

"You shouldn't have done that! He's under, just under!"

Of course! In his wool-gathering, Bain had nearly forgotten this girl ever had a husband. He muttered something awkward, in his contrition: "I thought . . . with the leaves about, and everything so neglected, you know . . . I thought no one would have been laid there this century."

She was calmer now, and they re-entered the house through the kitchen door. "I know. They shouldn't have put anyone there, after all this time. His uncle and grandfather are in the kirkyard in the village, and his two cousins. But he had himself buried in the old crypt; he wrote it into his will. Do you understand why? Because he knew I'd loathe it. I think tea will be ready, Captain Bain."

At the tea table, in a pleasant corner room of one tower, she was cool and even witty. Bain saw in her a girl become woman in some short space, a year or two, perhaps; she was charming and possibly wise. But something stirred woefully, now and again, beneath this pretty surface. The afternoon went rapidly and smoothly. When it was time for Bain to leave, she went with him to the great door; and she said, deliberately, "Come to tea tomorrow, too, if you like."

Startled, Bain hesitated; and she caught him up, with just the hint of a flash in her eyes, before he had said anything. "But don't trouble, Captain Bain, if you're to be busy."

"I'm never busy, Mrs. Lurlin," he told her, unable to repress his old arrogant grin. "Shall I be frank? I was surprised that you should ask me. I'm thoroughly *déclassé*."

She looked at him steadily. "I believe you're decent. I have no friends, and I hate to be solitary here, day on day. I'm afraid to be alone."

"I wouldn't take you to be timid, Mrs. Lurlin."

"Don't you understand? I thought you'd guessed." She

came a trifle closer to Bain; and she said, in her low sweet voice, "I'm afraid of my husband."

Bain stared at her. "Your husband? I understood—I thought that he's dead."

"Quite," said Ann Lurlin.

Somewhere in that Minoan maze of a house, a board or table creaked; the wind rattled a sash; and this little room at the stairfoot was musty. "You know, don't you?" Mrs. Lurlin whispered. "You know something's near."

* * *

Bain stayed on at the "King's Arms," and every afternoon he walked up the barren lawn to Sorworth Place for tea. Some days he came early, and with Mrs. Lurlin he tramped over the Muir of Sorworth, talking of books and queer corners and the small things of nature. Ann Lurlin, he perceived, was one of those women, now unhappily rare, who delight in knowing about squirrels' habits and in watching field mice and peeking into birds' nests, with a childlike curiosity quite insatiable.

On one afternoon, they reached the summit of the Law and looked back upon the Place. A vast twisted oak, still bare of new leaves, stood halfway between them and the house, its black branches outlined like fingers against the grey of the distant mansion. This was the finest of many brave views on the Muir of Sorworth, and they could see the colliery, a dismal smudge far down in the valley, and the red roofs of Sorworth village, at this remove still seeming the douce market town that it once had been. In the several days that had elapsed since Bain's first call, Mrs. Lurlin had not touched upon the theme of her parting shot at the stairfoot, and Bain had been content to let that field lie fallow. But now she clutched his arm, and he sensed that the mood was upon her again.

She was looking intently toward a rise of ground this side of the oak. "Do you—" She checked herself, and said, instead, "Do I seem rational to you, Captain?"

She did, he told her; but he said nothing of all the rest he felt about her.

"I am going to put your confidence to the test." He observed that her charming lips were pressed tightly together, when for a moment she was silent. "Do you think you see anything between us and that tree?"

Bain studied the face of the moor. At first he detected nothing; then, for just an instant, it seemed as if some large stooping creature had hurried from one hillock to another, perhaps its back showing above the bracken. "I don't know, Mrs. Lurlin," he said, a bit too quickly. "A dog?"

"It didn't seem like a dog to you, now, did it?" She looked into his eyes, and then turned her sleek head back toward the moor.

"No. I suppose it's a man out ferreting." But he let his inflexion rise toward the end of the sentence.

"No one keeps ferrets here, Captain Bain. I'm glad you saw it, too, because I feel less mad. But I don't think anyone else would have made it out. You saw it because you know me so well, and—and because of that crack in your poor head, perhaps. I fancy it makes you sensitive to certain things."

Bain thought it kindest to be blunt: he asked her what way she was rowing.

"Let's sit down here on the heather, then," she went on,

"where we can see for a good way round. I'd rather not talk about this when we're in the house. First I ought to say something about my husband."

Perceiving that all this hurt her, Bain murmured that he had been told her late husband had been no credit to the family.

"No," said Ann Lurlin, "*no*. Have you read Trollope, Captain? Perhaps you remember how he describes Sir Florian, in *The Eustace Diamonds*. Sir Florian Eustace had only two flaws—'he was vicious, and he was dying.' Now Lizzie Eustace married Florian knowing these things; but I didn't know them about my husband when I married. I hadn't any money, and no relative left worth naming. Alastair—though he looked sick, even then—had manners. I don't suppose I wanted to look very closely. Afterward, I found he was foul."

Bain dug his fingers into the heather.

"If we were to walk down toward that tree," said Mrs. Lurlin, after a silence, "I don't think we'd meet anything, not yet. I don't believe there's any—any *body* to what we saw. I fancy it was only a kind of presentiment. I've been alone here, more than once, and caught a glimpse of something and made myself hunt; but nothing ever was there."

"Supposing a thing like that could—could rise," Bain interjected, stealthily surveying the bracken, "why should he have power over you? You're not foul."

She did not seem to hear him. "He wanted everything to be vile, and me to be vilest of all. Sometimes I think it was the pain of dying in him that made him try to befoul everything. When he found he couldn't break me, he cursed like a devil, really as if he were in hell. But I stayed with him, to his last day; I was his wife, whatever he was. Most of the time he lay with his eyes shut, only gasping; but in the evening, when he was nearly gone, I could see he was trying to speak, and I bent down, and he smirked and whispered to me, 'You think you've won free, Ann? No. Wait a year. I'll want you then.' "

"A year?" asked Bain.

"It will be a year next Friday. Now I'm going to confess something." She turned her lithe body so that her eyes looked directly into Bain's. "When I saw you in the square, I wondered if I could use you. I had some notion that I might stick a life between myself and . . . You looked no better than a daredevil. Do you mind my saying that? Something in me whispered, 'He was made to take chances; that's what he's good for.' I meant you to come to see me. I don't suppose it flatters you, Ralph, to have been snared by a madwoman."

"No," Bain answered her. "You're not mad. We both may be dolls in someone's dream, Ann, but you're not mad."

"And you'd best go, for good," she told him. "I don't want to stain you with this, now that I know you. I want you to go away."

"You can't dismiss me," Bain contrived to grin his old grin. "I'm in your net. But how am I to get into your mind, Ann? How am I to stand between you and what your memory calls up?"

"If it were only memory and fancy, I could bear it." She shut her eyes. "A glimpse of him in a dream, a trick of imagination when I turn a dark corner, the shape dodging on the moor—those might pass away. But I think he's coming . . . Now you'll know I'm fit for Bedlam. I think he's coming—well, in the flesh, or something like."

"Nonsense!" said Bain.

"Very well, then, I'm mad. But you'll bear with me, Ralph? Perhaps something in me calls him; possibly I even control him, after a fashion. But I think he'll be here Friday night."

Believing she might faint, Bain put his big hand behind her head. "If you really think that, Ann, leave the house, and we'll go to Edinburgh or London or where you like. We'll leave now."

"Where could I live?" She nodded toward the grey castle. "It's all I have—not even enough to pay my rent anywhere else. And then, it would make no difference. I think he'd follow me. He wants life to drag down with him. Either he must break me, or he must be broken somehow himself, before he'll rest."

Bain sat awhile, and presently asked, "Do you want me to watch in Sorworth Place on Friday night, Ann?"

She turned away her head, as if ashamed of her selfishness. "I do."

It passed through his mind that she might think he was making a rake's bargain with her, over this wild business. A bargain he might have made with another woman, or even with this one at another time, he admitted to himself, but not with a woman beside herself with terror. "You understand, Ann," he blurted, "that I'm asking nothing of you, not now."

"I know," she whispered, her face still averted. "I'm offering nothing—nothing but your death of fright." Then she tried to laugh. "Who'd think, to look at you, Captain Bain, that you're so very proper? I'd rather be scandalous than damned."

Thus it was settled; and though they two walked and talked and drank their tea on the Tuesday and the Wednesday and the Thursday, they did not mention again her past or their future. Whatever sighed in some passage or cupboard of that old house, whatever shifted and faded across the moor—why, such intimations they ignored, speaking instead of the whaups that cried from the sky above them or of the stories they had loved as children.

* * *

Old Sorworth Place still was fit to stand a siege, Bain told himself as he mounted the staircase between the turrets on Friday afternoon. The lower windows could not be forced, the doors were immensely stout; anything that had substance might scrape and pound in vain outside, all night, once the bolts were shot home. Ann Lurlin herself admitted him, and they went to sit in her little study, and the hours fled, and their tea, untasted, grew cold; and at length they heard fat Margaret shuffle down the kitchen passage, open the door, and make her way through the policies toward the distant sanctuary of her son's cottage.

Then Ann's eyes seconded Bain's glance, and he ran down the stair to the kitchen door, locked it, and made sure the great door was well bolted. He returned to the study and the pale girl with the great black eyes. The night was coming on. They could think of very little to say. Here was Bain locked in for the night with the woman that he most desired, though he had known many women, too well. "Yet Tantalus' be his delight . . ." Unless she sought him, he would not touch her, in this her hour of dismay.

"Where will you stay?" asked Bain, when the sun had sunk quite below the level of the little west window of the study.

"In my bedroom," she said, drearily enough. "There's no place safer."

Her room was in the southern tower. Bain's mind reviewed the plan of the Place. "Is there a way into the tower except through the great hall?"

She shook her sweet head. "There were doors on the other levels, once, but they were blocked long ago."

This made his work easier. "Well, then, Ann, your bogle will have to swallow me whole before he opens the door behind the hanging, and I'm a sour morsel." He didn't admit the possibility of fleshly revenants, Bain told himself, and if he could keep her safe from frenzy this one night, she might be safe forever after.

Solemn as a hanging judge, she looked at him for what seemed a long time. "You shouldn't stay here, Ralph; I shouldn't have let you." She ran her little tongue along her dry lips. "You know I never can be anything to you." This was said with a kind of frozen tenderness.

These words hurt him beyond belief; and yet he had expected them. He saw himself as if in a mirror: his shallow, tired, defiant face, his frayed clothes, every long lazy inch of himself, futile and fickle. "No," said Bain, managing a hoarse laugh, "no, Ann, of course you can't—or not tonight. I meant to sit outside your door."

Biting her lip, she murmured, "Not tonight, nor any other night, ever."

"Well," Bain said, "you needn't drive the point home with a hammer. Besides, you might care for me in better days."

She continued to look at him as if beseeching mercy. "You don't understand me, Ralph. It's not you: why, so far as I still can care for any man, I care for you. Anyway, I'm grateful to you as I've never been to anyone else, and I'd give myself to you if I could. It's not what you think. It's this: after having a year with him, I couldn't bear to be anything to a man again. It would be dreadful. I can't forget."

"Don't tell yourself that." Bain spoke slowly and heavily. "It won't be true. Given time, this night and your life with that—that fellow will wash away. But I suppose I'll be gone, and good riddance."

She lit a candle: paraffin lamps and candles were the only lighting in the Place. Now, he knew, their night of listening and guarding must commence. "You still can go, Ralph," she told him, softly. "A moment ago I hinted that I felt something for you, but that was because I tried to be kind. Kind! Well, whatever makes you do this for me? In honesty, I don't love you, though I should."

"Bravado," Bain said, "and boredom, mixed." He was glad she could not see his eyes or his mouth in that feeble candlelight. "Now up with you, and let me play my game of hide-and-seek, Ann Lurlin." He went with her to the door behind the hanging, and watched her ascend to the first turn of the stair. Looking back upon him, she contrived a smile of understanding, and was gone to her room. Alone, he felt a swelling of confidence.

"Come on, if you like, Alastair Lurlin, Esq.," he thought. "I'm your man for a bout of creep-mouse."

Before settling himself in the hall for the night, he must make sure that no one was playing tricks, a remote possibility he had kept at the back of his mind, by way of a forlorn link with the world of solid things. So, taking his little electric torch from a pocket, he proceeded to inspect every chill corner of the Place, apart from Ann's south tower, with a military thoroughness. Certain corners in this pile were calculated to make one wary; but they were empty, every one. After half an hour or so, he found himself looking from a loophole in the north tower, and across the main block of the house he saw a light glowing from Ann's window. There she would be lying in a passion of dread. But nothing should force itself upon her this night.

Returning to the main block, he listened: nothing. "For a parson's son," he thought, "Ralph Bain gets into peculiar nooks." Then he opened a door into the great hall.

O God! Something white was by the stair door, even then slipping out of the hall into the turret. He flung himself across the hall, down the stair, and leaped the last twist of the spiral to overtake that white fugitive. It was Ann Lurlin, pressing herself against the great door.

She shuddered there in her nightgown, her slim naked feet upon the damp flagstones. For a tremulous instant he thought his own desperate longing might have stirred some impulse in her: that she might have come to him out of love or gratitude. But a glance at her face undid his hope. She was nearly out of her mind, a tormented thing fumbling at the oak, and when he took her by the arms, she panted spasmodically and managed to say, "I don't know why I'm here. I wanted to run out, run and run."

For only a moment he pressed her body to his. Then,

picking her up, he carried her to the door behind the hanging, and thrust her in. "Go back, Ann: I've promised you." She put both her chill hands in his, looked at him as if she were to paint his picture, and kissed him lightly with cold lips. Then she crept up the steps. He bolted the little tapestried door from his side.

Well, back to sentry-duty. What hadn't he inspected in this house? The cellars. Down you go, Captain Bain. They were fine old Scots vaults of flinty stone, those cellars, but he detested them this night. Outside, a light rain was falling. He sat upon a broken stool in the cellar that had been a medieval kitchen, shadowed by the protruding oven. This was the ragtaggle end of chivalry all right—a worn-out fool crouching in a crumbling house to humor a crazy girl. Then something crunched on the gravel outside the barred window. From old-soldierly habit, Bain kept stock-still in the shadow.

He saw it plain, so that there could be no possibility of illusion; and he asked himself, in a frantic sensation of which he was at once ashamed, "What have you got into, Ralph Bain, for the sake of a pretty little thing that won't be yours?"

It was a face at the slit of a window, damn it: a sickening face, the nose snubbed against the glass like a little boy's at a sweetshop. The eyelids of this face were drawn down; but while Bain watched, they slowly opened, as if drawn upward by a power beyond themselves, and the face turned awkwardly upon its neck, surveying the cellar. Somehow Bain knew, with an immense temporary relief, that he was not perceived in his sanctuary back of the oven, supposing the thing could "perceive" in any ordinary sense. Then the face withdrew from the window, and again Bain heard the gravel crunch.

Some little time elapsed before Bain could make his muscles obey him. The crunching grew fainter, and then, hearing with a preternatural acuity, he made out a fumbling at the small kitchen door down the passage. But it was a vain fumbling. Something groped, lifted the latch, pressed its weight against the barrier. The stout door did not budge. At this, Bain experienced a reckless exultation: whatever was outside in the night obeyed in some sort the laws of matter. "Go on, you dead hands," thought Bain, wildly. "Fumble, damn you, push, scratch like a cat. You'll not get at her." Rising from his stool, Bain tiptoed down the passage, and heard the stumbling feet in the gravel, moving on. Would it try the big door? Of course. Let it try.

Bain told himself he had to look at what was outside; and he made his way to the lowest loophole of the left-hand turret, which commanded the steps. There was moon enough to show him the stairs, and they were empty. But the great door, a trifle ajar, was just closing *behind* whatever had entered.

He sucked in his breath, and believed he would go mad. "O Lord! O Lord! It's in, and I'm done for!" These phrases thrust through his consciousness like hot needles. Yet a dogged rationality contended against them. However had the door been forced? Then he thought of Ann in her nightgown. Before he had caught her, she must have drawn the bolt; and he, in his love-sick anxiety, had forgotten to try it. Collusion between the living and the damned: this conjecture of treachery woke in him, and he felt momentarily that all his days with Ann Lurlin had been part of a witch's snare. But he rejected the doubt. Whatever had moved Ann, whether simple terror and a foolish hope of flight, or some blind impulse forced upon her out of the abyss, no deceit lay in her.

These sterile reflections occupied no mensurable time. Face it out, Bain: nothing else for it. With luck, he could be in the hall first. He was up the kitchen stair and through an anteroom as fast as ever he had moved in his life. An uncertain moonlight showed him the hall, and he was alone in it, barring the way to the tapestried door; but then the door from the turret stair opened. Something entered.

Just inside the hall, the thing paused heavily. Light enough came from the great window to outline it; Bain had not the heart to pull out his torch; indeed, he could not move at all. Again he looked upon the sagging face he had seen at the cellar-loop. The thing was clothed in a black suit, all mildewed. Its slow body seemed to gather itself for new movement.

Who should be master, who should move first—these points might decide the issue, Bain hoped: perhaps a horrid logic governed this contest. Ralph Bain then compelled himself to take two steps forward, toward the middle of the hall. He looked at the dark shape by the window, and twice tried to speak, and on the third attempt a few broken words croaked from his throat: "Time you were properly buried, old man."

No answering sound came. Bain flexed his arms, but could not force himself to advance further. He could discern no expression upon the face: only a blackened mask obedient to some obscene impulse from a remote beyond. How long they two stood there, Bain did not know. But presently the thing swung about awkwardly, lurched over the threshold, and was gone back to the darkness of the stair-turret.

Bain thanked God with all sincerity. Now who was the hunter and who the quarry? The will was in him to make an end of this thing. Would it have gone back to the door and out into the rain? Bain listened. Yes, there came a stumbling on the stair—from above. What was it trying for? And then Bain knew. Ah, what a fool he was! It was ascending to the roofs, and would cross the slabs to the woman whose passionate terror perhaps animated its shape.

Bain went after it, slipping and bruising himself in his urgency; but as he leaped up the spiral toward the higher stories of the north tower, he felt a cold draught sweeping down upon him. The thing had got open a window, and must be upon the roof. Bain found that window, and stared into the night.

Now the rain fell heavily, and down at the foot of the wall, Sorworth Water moaned and gleamed. From Ann Lurlin's room, the candlelight cast some faint radiance upon the stone slabs of the sharp-peaked roof; and the glimmer was enough to show Bain a sodden bulk inching its way along the gutter toward the south tower, a footing precarious enough in daylight. The ruined face was averted from Bain, whatever power moved the thing being intent upon that piteous lighted window.

What propelled Ralph Bain then was an impulse beyond duty, beyond courage, beyond even the love of woman. He dropped from the window upon the wet and shimmering slabs, clambered along the gutter, and flung himself upon the dark hulk. Bain heaved with all the strength that was in him. Together, living and dead, they rolled upon the mossy old stones; together they fell.

A glimpse of the great stone wall; a flash of the savage burn; then explosion of everything, opening to the blessed dark.

*   *   *

Early on Saturday morning, a lone fisherman out of Sorworthness, rowing near the reefs that lie off the mouth of Sorworth Water, thought he perceived some unpleasant mass lying nearly submerged in the tangle of kelp among the rocks. But the sea boils nastily there, and the fisherfolk of Sorworthness are of the old legend-cherishing sort, and this man recalled certain things muttered by the arthritic old hag in the chimney corner, his mother. Rather than rowing closer in, then, he worked his boat round and made back toward the decayed little harbor.

Some hours later, having got two friends into his boat for company, he returned to the skerries for a closer look; but the tide had ebbed, and if anything human or human-like had lodged earlier among the rocks, now it was gone forever. Whatever ends in the boiling sea upon the reefs, having tumbled down the den of Sorworth Water, never wakes again.

BEHIND THE STUMPS

♤

"And Satan stood up against Israel,
and provoked David to number Israel."

Pottawattomie County, shorn of its protecting forest seventy years ago, ever since has sprawled like Samson undone by Delilah, naked, impotent, grudgingly servile. Amid the fields of rotted stumps potatoes and beans grow, and half the inhabited houses still are log cabins thrown up by the lumbermen who followed the trappers into this land. In Pottawattomie there has been no money worth mentioning since the timber was cut; but here and there people cling to the straggling farms, or makeshift in the crumbling villages.

An elusive beauty drifts over this country sprinkled with little lakes, stretches of second-growth woods and cedar swamps, gravelly upland ridges that are gnawed by every rain, now that their cover is gone. As if a curse had been pronounced upon these folk and their houses and their crops in reprisal for their violation of nature, everything in Pottawattomie is melting away.

Of the people who stick obstinately to this stump-country, some are grandchildren and great-grandchildren of the men who swept off the forest; others are flotsam cast upon these sandy miles from the torrent of modern life, thrown out of the eddy upon the soggy bank to lie inert and ignored. Worn farmers of a conservative cast of mind, pinched, tenacious, inured to monotony, fond of the bottle on Saturday nights; eccentrics of several sorts; a silent half-breed crew of Negro-and-Indian, dispersed in cabins and sun-stricken tar-paper shanties along the back roads, remote from the county seat and the lesser hamlets that conduct the languid commerce of Pottawattomie—these are the Pottawattomie people. Decent roads have come only lately; even television is too costly for many of these folk; the very hand of government is nerveless in this poverty of soil and spirit.

Yet not wholly palsied, the grip of the State, for all that. Tax assessments necessarily are modest in Pottawattomie, but there are highways to be maintained, poaching of deer and trout to be repressed, old age relief to be doled out. There exists a sheriff, intimate with the local tone, at the county seat; also a judge of probate; and the county supervisors are farmers and tradesmen without inclination to alter the nature of things in Pottawattomie. So far, government is a shadow of a shade. But now and again the State administration and the Federal administration gingerly poke about in the mud and brush of the stump-land.

A special rural census had to be compiled. Down in the capital, a plan had been drawn up concerning commodity

Behind the Stumps 171

price-levels and potential crop yields and tabulated prices. Acres of corn were to be counted, and pigs and people. Enumerators went out to every spreading wheat farm, to every five-acre tomato patch; and Pottawattomie County was not forgotten.

Always against the government, Pottawattomie; against the administration that ordained this special census, most vehemently. This new survey, Pottawattomie declared, meant more blank forms, more trips to the county seat, higher taxation, and intolerable prying into every man's household—which last none resent more than do the rural poor.

So the Regional Office of the Special Census began to encounter difficulties in Pottawattomie. Doors were shut in the faces of certified enumerators, despite threats of warrants and writs; the evasive response was common, violent reaction not inconceivable. Reports particularly unsettling were received from the district of Bear City, a decayed village of two hundred inhabitants. Despite his pressing need for the stipend attached to the office, the temporary agent there resigned in distress at a growing unpopularity. A woman who took his place was ignored by half the farmers she endeavored to interview.

Put out, the Regional Office dispatched to Bear City a Special Interviewer: Cribben. They let him have a car and a stack of forms and rather a stiff letter of introduction to the postmaster in that town, and off he drove northward.

Being that sort of man, Cribben took his revolver with him. Once he had been a bank messenger, and he often told his associates, "The other messengers carried their guns at the bottom of their brief cases, so there'd be no chance of having to pull them if there was a stick-up. But I kept my .38 handy. I was willing to have it out with the boys."

Tall, forty, stiff as a stick, this Cribben—walking with chin up, chest out, joints rigid, in a sort of nervous defiance of humanity. He looked insufferable. He was insufferable. Next to a jocular man, an insufferable man is best suited for the responsibilities that are a Special Interviewer's. Close-clipped black hair set off a strong head, well proportioned; but the mouth was petulant, and the eyes were ignorantly challenging, and the chin was set in lines of pomposity. In conversation, Cribben had a way of sucking in his cheeks with an affectation of whimsical deliberation, for Cribben had long told himself that he was admirably funny when he chose to be, especially with women. Years before, his wife had divorced him—in Reno, since (somewhat to her bewilderment) she had been able to think of no precise ground which would admit of obtaining a divorce in their own state. He lived chastely, honestly, soberly, quite solitary. He laughed dutifully at other men's jokes; he would go out of his way to write a friendly letter of recommendation; but somehow no one ever asked him out or looked him up. A failure in everything was Cribben—ex-engineer, ex-chief clerk, ex-artillery captain, ex-foundry partner. He told himself he had been completely reliable in every little particular, which was true; and he told himself he had failed because of his immaculate honesty in a mob of rogues, which was false. He had failed because he was precise.

"Corporal, about the morning report: I see you used eraser to clean up this ink blot, instead of correction fluid. Watch that, Corporal. We'll use correction fluid. Understand?" This is the sort of thing the precise Cribben would say—if with a smile, then the wrong kind of smile; and he would compliment himself on his urbanity.

Cribben did not spare himself; no man ever was more methodical, more painstaking. Reliable in every little particular, yes; but so devoted to these particulars that generalities went to pot. Subordinates resigned and read the "help wanted" columns rather than submit to another week of such accuracy; superiors found him hopelessly behind in his work, austerely plodding through tidy inconsequentialities. Truly, Cribben was intolerable. He knew the mass of men to be consistently inaccurate and often dishonest. Quite right, of course. Sensible men nod and shrug; Cribben nagged. His foundry went to pieces because he fretted about missing wrenches and screwdrivers. He thought his workmen stole them. They did; but Cribben never would confess that moderate pilferage was an item of fixed overhead. In Cribben's pertinacity there would have been something noble, had he loved precision for the sake of truth. But he regarded truth only as an attribute of precision.

So down to that sink of broken men, petty governmental service, spun Cribben in the vortex of failure. Having arrived at the abyss, which in this instance was a temporary junior clerkship, Cribben commenced to rise in a small way. In this humorless precision the assistant chief of the Regional Office discerned the very incarnation of the second-best type of public functionary, and so set him to compelling the reluctant to complete interminable forms. Cribben became a Special Investigator, with every increase of salary authorized by statute. To entrust him with supervisory duties proved inadvisable; yet within his sphere, Cribben was incomparable. It was Cribben's apotheosis. Never had he liked work so well, and only a passion to reorganize the Regional Office upon a more precise model clouded his contentment. With the majesty of Government at his back, the hauteur of a censor in his mien as he queried the subject of a survey or interrogated the petitioner for a grant—a man like Cribben never dreamed of more than this. For Cribben was quite devoid of imagination.

And Cribben drove north to Bear City.

False-fronted dry goods shops and grocery stores and saloons, built lavishly of second-grade white pine when pine was cheap and seemingly inexhaustible, are strung along a broad gravelled road: this is Bear City. They are like discolored teeth in an old man's mouth, these buildings, for they stand between grass-grown gaps where casual flames have had their way with abandoned structures. One of these shops, with the usual high, old-fashioned windows and siding a watery white, is also the post office. On Saturday afternoons in little places like this, post offices generally close. But on this Saturday afternoon, in Bear City—so Cribben noted as he parked his automobile—not only the dry goods half of the shop, but the post office too was open for business. This was tidy and efficient, Cribben reflected, striding through the door. It predisposed him to amiability.

"Afternoon," said Cribben to the postmaster. "I'm J. K. Cribben, from the Regional Office. Read this, please." He presented his letter of introduction.

Mr. Matt Heddle, Postmaster, Bear City, was behind the wrought-iron grill of the old post office counter, a relic of earlier days and more southerly towns; and his shy wife Jessie was opposite, at the shop counter. They were not lacking in a dignity that comes from honorable posts long held in small places. Mr. Heddle, with his crown of thick white hair and his august slouch, his good black suit, and his deep slow voice, made a rural postmaster for one to be proud of.

"Why, I wish you luck, Mr. Cribben," Matt Heddle said with concern, reading the letter of introduction. Mr. Heddle desired to be postmaster for the rest of his life. "I'll do anything I can. I'm sorry about the fuss the other census man had."

"His own damned fault," Cribben said, largely. "Don't give a grouch a chance to make a fuss—that's my way. Take none of their lip. I've handled people quite awhile. Shoot out your questions, stare 'em down. I won't have much trouble here."

He didn't. Whatever Cribben's shortcomings, he was neither coward nor laggard. Only six or seven hours a day he spent in the tourist room he had rented; and by the time six days had passed, he had seen and conquered almost all the obdurate farmers around Bear City. Their sheds and their silos, their sheep and their steers, their hired men and their bashful daughters, the rooms in their houses and the privies behind them—all were properly observed and recorded in forms and check-sheets. What Cribben could not see with his own eyes he bullied out adequately enough from the uneasy men he cornered and glowered upon. He was big, he was gruff, he was pedantically insistent. He was worth what salary the Regional Office paid. He never took "no" for an answer—or "don't know," either. He made himself detested in Bear City more quickly than ever had man before; and he paid back his contemners in a condescending scorn.

His success was the product, in part, of his comparative restraint: for he seemed to those he confronted to be holding himself precariously in check, on the verge of tumbling into some tremendous passion, like a dizzy man teetering on a log across a stream in spate. He was cruelly cold, always—never fierce, and yet hanging by a worn rope. What brute would have had the callousness, or the temerity, to thrust this man over the brink? It was safer to answer his questions and endure his prying.

Over the rutted trails of Pottawattomie County in muddy spring he drove his official automobile, finding out every shack and hut, every Indian squatter, every forlorn old couple back in the cedar thickets, every widow who boasted a cow and a chicken run. They were numbered, all numbered. This spring the birds were thick in Pottawattomie and some of the lilacs bloomed early, but Cribben never looked at them, for they were not to be enumerated. He had not an ounce of fancy in him. Six days of this and he had done the job except for the Barrens. Of all Pottawattomie, Bear City district was the toughest nut for the Special Census, and the Barrens were the hard kernel of Bear City's hinterland.

Who lives in the Barrens, that sterile and gullied and scrub-veiled upland? Why, it's hard to say. A half-dozen scrawny families, perhaps more—folk seldom seen, more seldom heard, even in Bear City. They have no money for the dissipations of a town, the Barrens people—none of them, at least, except the Gholsons; and no one ever knew a Gholson to take a dollar out of his greasy old purse for anything but a sack of sugar or a bottle of rot-gut whisky.

The Gholsons must have money, as money goes in Pottawattomie, but it sticks to them.

On Saturday afternoon, a week after his arrival in town, Cribben entered the post office, self-satisfied and muddy. Matt Heddle was there, and Love the garage-man—Love already lively from morning libations. "Started on the Barrens this morning, Heddle," Cribben said ponderously. "Easy as falling off a log. Covered the Robinson place, and Hendry's. Eight kids at the Robinsons', dirty as worms." He looked at his map. "Tomorrow, now, I begin with this place called Barrens Mill. Not much of a road into it. It's right on Owens Creek. What d'you know about Barrens Mill, Heddle?" He pointed, his heavy forefinger stiff, at a spot on his map.

Mr. Matt Heddle was a good-natured old man, but he did not like Cribben. Pottawattomie people said that Mr. Heddle was well read, which in Pottawattomie County means that a man has three reprints of Marie Corelli's novels and two of Hall Caine's, but they were not far wrong in Heddle's case. The appetite for knowledge clutched at him as it sometimes does at pathetic men past their prime, and his devotion to the better nineteenth century novelists, combining with some natural penetration, had made him shrewd enough. His good nature being unquenchable, he looked at grim Cribben and thought he read in that intolerant face a waste of loneliness and doubt that Cribben never could confess to himself, for terror of the desolation.

He looked at Cribben, and told him: "Let it go, Mr. Cribben. They're an ignorant bunch, the Gholsons; they own Barrens Mill. Let it go. It'll be knee-deep in mud up there. Look up the acreage in the county office, and the assessment, and let it go at that. You've done all the work anybody could ask."

"We don't let things go in the Regional Office," Cribben said, with austerity. "I've already looked in the county book: five hundred and twenty acres the Gholsons own. But I want to know *what* Gholson."

Matt Heddle started to speak, hesitated, looked speculatively at Cribben, and then said, "It's Will Gholson that pays the taxes."

Love, who had been leaning against the counter, a wise grin on his face, gave a whisky chuckle and remarked, abruptly: "She was a witch and a bitch, a bitch and a witch. Ha! Goin' to put *her* in the census?"

"Dave Love, this isn't the Elite; it's the post office," Mr. Heddle said, civilly. "Let's keep it decent in here."

"Yes, Will Gholson pays the taxes," Cribben nodded, "but the land's not in his name. The tax-roll reads 'Mrs. Gholson'—just that. No Christian name. How do you people choose your county clerk?"

"Mrs. Gholson, old Bitch Gholson, old Witch Gholson," chanted Love. "You goin' to put *her* in the census? She's dead as a dodo."

"Will Gholson's mother, maybe, or his grandmother—that's who's meant," Heddle murmured. "Nobody really knows the Gholsons. They aren't folks you get to know. They're an ignorant bunch, good to keep clear of. She was old, old. I saw her laid out. Some of us went up there for the funeral—only time we ever went inside the house. It was only decent to go up."

"Decent, hell!" said Love. "We was scared not to go,

that's the truth of it. Nobody with any brains rubs the Gholsons the wrong way."

"Scared?" Cribben sneered down at Love.

"God, yes, man. She was a damned witch, and the whole family's bats in the belfry. Old Mrs. Gholson have a Christian name? Hell, whoever heard of a witch with a Christian name?"

"You start your drinking too early in the day," Cribben said. Love snorted, grinned, and fiddled with a post-office pen. "What kind of a county clerk do you have, Heddle, that doesn't take a dead woman's name off the books?"

"Why, I suppose maybe the Gholsons wanted it left on," Heddle sighed, placatingly. "And there was talk. Nobody wants to fuss with the Gholsons. Sleeping dogs, Mr. Cribben."

"If you really want to know," Love growled, "she cursed the cows, for one thing. The cows of people she didn't care for, and the neighbors that were too close. The Gholsons don't like close neighbors."

"What are you giving me?" Cribben went menacingly red at the idea of being made the butt of a joke: this was the one thing his humorless valor feared.

"You don't have to believe it, man, but the cows went dry, all the same. And sometimes they died. And if that wasn't enough, the Gholsons moved the fences, and the boundary-markers. They took over. They got land now that used to be four or five farms."

Mrs. Heddle, having been listening, now came across the shop to say in her shy voice, "They did move the posts, Mr. Cribben—the Gholsons. And the neighbors didn't move them back. They were frightened silly."

"It'll take more than a sick cow to scare me, Mrs. Heddle," Cribben told her, the flush fading from his cheeks. "You people don't have any system up here. What's wrong with your schools, that people swallow this stuff? How do you hire your teachers?"

"Barrens Mill is a place to put a chill into a preacher, Mr. Cribben," said Matt Heddle, meditatively. "There's a look to it . . . the mill itself is gone, but the big old house is there, seedy now, and the rest of the buildings. John Wendover, the lumberman, built it when this country was opened up, but the Gholsons bought it after the timber went. Some people say the Gholsons came from Missouri. I don't know. There's stories . . . Nobody knows the Gholsons. They've another farm down the creek. There's five Gholson men, nowadays, but I don't know how many women. Will Gholson does the talking for them, and he talks as much as a clam."

"He'll talk to me," Cribben declared.

Over Matt Heddle came a sensation of pity. Leaning across the counter, he put his hand on Cribben's. Few ever had done this, and Cribben, startled, stepped back. "Now, listen, Mr. Cribben, friend. You're a man with spunk, and you know your business; but I'm old, and I've been hereabouts a while. There are people that don't fit in anywhere, Mr. Cribben. Did you ever think about that? I mean, they won't live by your ways and mine. Some of them are too good, and some are too bad. Everybody's growing pretty much alike—nearly everybody—in this age, and the one's that don't fit in are scarce; but they're still around. Some are queer, very queer. We can't just count them like so many four-cent stamps. We can't change them, not soon.

But they're shy, most of them: let them alone, and they're likely to crawl into holes, out of the sun. Let them be; they don't signify, if you don't stir them up. The Gholsons are like that."

"They come under the law, same as anybody else," Cribben put in.

"Oh, the law was made for you and me and the folks we know—not for them, any more than it was made for snakes. So long as they let the law alone, don't meddle, Mr. Cribben, don't meddle. They don't signify any more than a wasps' nest at the back of the orchard, if you don't poke them." Old Heddle was very earnest.

"A witch of a bitch and a bitch of a witch," sang Love, mordantly. "O Lord, how she hexed 'em!"

"Why, there's Will Gholson now, coming out of the Elite," Mrs. Heddle whispered from the window. A greasy, burly man with tremendous eyebrows that had tufted points was walking from the bar with a bottle in either hip-pocket. He was neither bearded nor shaven, and he was filthy. He turned toward a wagon hitched close by the post office.

"Handsome specimen," observed Cribben, chafing under all this admonition, the defiance in his lonely nature coming to a boil. "We'll have a talk." He strode into the street, Matt Heddle anxiously behind him and Love sauntering in the rear. Gholson, sensing them, swung round from tightening his horse's harness. Unquestionably he was a rough customer; but that roused Cribben's spirit.

"Will Gholson," called out Cribben in his artillery-captain voice, "I've got a few questions to ask you."

A stare; and then Gholson spat into the road. His words

were labored, a heavy blur of speech, like a man wrestling with a tongue uncongenial to him. "You the counter?"

"That's right," Cribben told him. "Who owns your farm, Gholson?"

Another stare, longer, and a kind of slow, dismal grimace. "Go to hell," said Gholson. "Leave us be."

Something about this earth-stained, sweat-reeking figure, skulking on the frontier of humanity, sent a stir of revulsion through Cribben; and the consciousness of his inward shrinking set fire to his conceit, and he shot out one powerful arm to catch Gholson by the front of his tattered overalls. "By God, Gholson, I'm coming out to your place tomorrow; and I'm going through it; I'll have a warrant; and I'll do my duty; so watch yourself. I hear you've got a queer place at Barrens Mill, Gholson. Look out I don't get it condemned for you." Cribben was white, from fury, and shouting like a sailor, and shaking in his emotion. Even the dull lump of Gholson's face lost its apathy before this rage, and Gholson stood quiescent in the tall man's grip.

"Mr. Cribben, friend," Heddle was saying. Cribben remembered where he was, and what; he let go of Gholson's clothes; but he put his drawn face into Gholson's and repeated, "Tomorrow. I'll be out tomorrow."

"Tomorrow's Sunday," was all Gholson answered.

"I'll be there tomorrow."

"Sunday's no day for it," said Gholson, almost plaintively. It was as if Cribben had stabbed through this hulk of flesh and rasped upon a moral sensibility.

"I'll be there," Cribben told him, in grim triumph.

Deliberately Gholson got into his wagon, took up the reins, and paused as if collecting his wits for a weighty effort. "Don't, Mister." It was a grunt. "A man that—a man that fusses on Sunday—well, he deserves what he gets." And Gholson drove off.

"What's wrong, Mr. Cribben?" asked Heddle, startled: for Cribben had slipped down upon the bench outside the post office and was sucking in his breath convulsively. "Here, a nip," said Love, in concern, thrusting a bottle at him. Cribben took a swallow of whisky, sighed, and relaxed. He drew an envelope out of a pocket and swallowed a capsule, with another mouthful of whisky.

"Heart?" asked Heddle.

"Yes," Cribben answered, as humbly as was in him. "It never was dandy. I'm not supposed to get riled."

"With that heart, you don't want to go up to Barrens Mill—no, you don't," said the postmaster, gravely.

"She's a witch, Cribben." Love was leaning over him. "Hear me, eh? I say, she *is* a witch."

"Quiet, Love," the postmaster told him. "Or if you do go to the Barrens, Mr. Cribben, you'll take a couple of the sheriff's boys with you."

Cribben had quite intended to ask for a deputy, but he'd be damned now if he wouldn't go alone. "I'm driving to the judge for a search warrant," he answered, his chin up. "That's all I'll take."

Heddle walked with him to the boardinghouse where Cribben kept his automobile. He said nothing all the way, but when Cribben had got behind the wheel, he leaned in the window, his big, smooth, friendly old face intent: "There's a lot of old-fashioned prejudice in Pottawattomie, Mr. Cribben. But, you know, most men run their lives on prejudice. We've got to; we're not smart enough to do anything else. There's sure to be something behind a prejudice. I don't know all about the Gholsons, but there's fact behind prejudice. Some things are best left alone."

Here Cribben rolled up his window and shook his head and started the motor and rolled off.

After all, there was no more he could have said, Matt Heddle reflected. Cribben would go to Barrens Mill, probably count everything in sight, and bullyrag Will Gholson, and come back puffed up like a turkey. Misty notions . . . He almost wished someone would put the fear of hell-fire into the Special Interviewer. But this was only an old-fangled backwater, and Cribben was a new-fangled man.

* * *

On Sunday morning, Cribben drove alone up the road toward the Barrens. In his pockets were a set of forms, and a warrant in case of need; Cribben left his gun at home, thinking the devil of a temper within him a greater hazard than any he was liable to encounter from the Gholsons. Past abandoned cabins and frame houses with their roofs fallen in, past a sluggish stream clogged with ancient logs, past mile on mile of straggling second-growth woodland, Cribben rode. It was empty country, not one-third so populous as it had been fifty years before, and he passed no one at this hour.

Here in the region of the Barrens, fence wire was unknown: enormous stumps, uprooted from the fields and dragged to the roadside, are crowded one against another to keep the cows out, their truncated roots pointing toward the empty sky. Most symbolic of the stump-country, jagged and dead, these fences; but Cribben had no time for myth.

By ten o'clock he was nursing his car over the remnant of a corduroy road which twists through Long Swamp; the stagnant water was a foot deep upon it, this spring. But he went through without mishap, only to find himself a little later snared in the wet ground between two treacherous sand hills. There was no traction for his rear wheels; maddened, he made them spin until he had sunk his car to the axle; and then, cooling, he went forward on foot. Love's Garage could pull out the automobile later; he would have to walk back to town, or find a telephone somewhere, when he was through with this business. He had promised to be at Barrens Mill that morning, and he would be there. Already he was within a mile of the farm.

The damp track that once had been a lumber road could have led him, albeit circuitously, to the Gholsons. But, consulting his map, Cribben saw that by walking through a stretch of hardwoods he could—with luck—save fifteen minutes' tramping. So up a gradual ascent he went, passing on his right the wreck of a little farmhouse with high gables, not many years derelict. "The Gholsons don't like close neighbors." Oaks and maples and beeches, this wood, with soggy leaves of many autumns underfoot and spongemushrooms springing up from them, clammily white. Water from the trees dripped upon Cribben, streaking his short coat. It was a quiet wood, most quiet; the dying vestige of a path led through it.

Terminating upon the crest of a ridge, the path took him to a stump fence of grand proportions. Beyond was pasture, cleared with a thoroughness exceptional in this country; and beyond the pasture, the ground fell away to a swift creek, and then rose again to a sharp knoll, of which the shoulder faced him; and upon the knoll was the house of Barrens Mill, a quarter of a mile distant.

All round the house stretched the Gholsons' fields, the work of years of fantastic labor. What power had driven these dull men to such feats of agricultural vainglory? For it was a beautiful farm: every dangerous slope affectionately buttressed and contoured to guard it from the rains, every boulder hauled away to a pile at the bend of the stream, every potential weed-jungle rooted out. The great square house—always severely simple, now gaunt in its blackened boards from which paint had scaled away long since—surveyed the whole rolling farm. A low wing, doubtless containing kitchen and woodshed, was joined to the northern face of the old building, which seemed indefinably mutilated. Then Cribben realized how the house had been injured: it was nearly blind. Every window above the ground-floor had been neatly boarded up—not covered over merely, but the frames taken out and planks fitted to fill the apertures. It was as if the house had fallen prisoner to the Gholsons, and sat Samson-like in bound and blindfolded shame.

All this was apprehended at a single glance; a second look disclosed nothing living in all the prospect—not even a dog, not even a cow. But one of the pallid stumps stirred.

Cribben started. No, not a stump: someone crouching by the stump fence, leaning upon a broken root, and watching, not him, but the house. It was a girl, barefoot, a few yards away, dressed in printed meal-sacks, fifteen or sixteen years old, and thoroughly ugly, her hair a rat's-nest; this was no country where a wild rose might bloom. She had not heard him. For all his ungainly ways, Cribben had spent a good deal of time in the open, and could be meticulously quiet. He stole close up to the girl and said, in a tone he meant to be affable, "Well, now?"

Ah, what a scream out of her! She had been watching the blind façade of Barrens Mill house with such a degree of intensity, a kind of cringing smirk on her lips, that Cribben's words must have come like the voice from the burning bush; and she whirled, and shrieked, all sense gone out of her face, until she began to understand that it was only a stranger by her. Though Cribben was not a feeling man, this extremity of fright touched him almost with compassion, and he took the girl gently by the shoulder, saying, "It's all right. Will you take me to the house?" He made as if to lead her down the slope.

At that, the tide of fright poured back into her heavy Gholson face, and she fought in his grasp and swore at him. Cribben—a vein of prudery ran through his nature—was badly shocked: it was hysterically vile cursing, nearly inarticulate, but compounded of every ancient rural obscenity. And she was very young. She pulled away and dodged into the dense wood.

Nothing moved in these broad fields. No smoke rose from the kitchen, no chickens cackled in the yard. Overhead a crow flapped, as much an alien as Cribben himself; nothing more seemed to live about Barrens Mill. Were Will Gholson crazy enough to be peering from one of the windows with a shotgun beside him, Cribben would make a target impossible to miss, and Cribben knew this. But no movement came from behind the blinds, and Cribben went round unscathed to the kitchen door.

A pause and a glance told Cribben that the animals were

gone, every one of them, to the last hen and the last cat. Driven down to the lower farm to vex and delay him? And it looked as if every Gholson had gone with them. He knocked at the scarred back door: only echoes. It was not locked; and, having his warrant in his pocket, he entered. If Will Gholson were keeping mum inside, he'd rout him out.

Four low rooms—kitchen, rough parlor, a couple of topsy-turvy bedrooms—this was the wing of the house, showing every sign of a hasty flight. A massive panelled door shut off the parlor from the square bulk of the older house, and its big key was in the lock. Well, it was worth a try. Cribben, unlocking the door, looked in: black, frayed blinds drawn down over the windows—and the windows upstairs boarded, of course. Returning to the kitchen, he got a kerosene lamp, lit it, and went back to the darkened rooms.

Fourteen-foot ceilings in these cold chambers; and the remnants of Victorian prosperity in mildewed love seats and peeling gilt mirrors; and dust, dust. A damp place, wholly still. Cribben, telling his nerves to behave, plodded up the fine sweep of the solid stairs, the white plaster of the wall gleaming from his lamp. Dust, dust.

A broad corridor, and three rooms of moderate size, their doors ajar, a naked bedstead in each; and at the head of the corridor, a door that stuck. The stillness infecting him, Cribben pressed his weight cautiously upon the knob, so that the squeak of the hinges was light when the door yielded. Holding the lamp above his head, he was in.

Marble-topped commode, washbowl holding a powder of grime, fantastic oaken wardrobe—and a tremendous Victorian rosewood bed, carven and scrolled, its towering head casting a shadow upon the sheets that covered the mattress. There *were* sheets; and they were humped with the shape of someone snuggled under them.

"Come on out," said Cribben, his throat dry. No one answered, and he ripped the covers back. He had a half-second to stare before he dropped the lamp to its ruin.

Old, old—how old? She had been immensely fat, he could tell in that frozen moment, but now the malign wrinkles hung in horrid empty folds. How evil! And even yet, that drooping lip of command, that projecting jaw—he knew at last from what source had come the power that terraced and tended Barrens Mill. The eyelids were drawn down. For this only was there time before the lamp smashed. Ah, why hadn't they buried her? For she was dead, long dead, many a season dead.

All light gone, Cribben stood rigid, his fingers pressed distractedly against his thighs. To his brain, absurdly, came a forgotten picture out of his childhood, a colored print in his *King Arthur:* "Launcelot in the Chapel of the Dead Wizard," with the knight lifting the corner of a shroud. This picture dropping away, Cribben told his unmoving self, silently but again and again, "Old Mrs. Gholson, old witch, old bitch," as if it were an incantation. Then he groped for the vanished door, but stumbled upon the wire guard of the broken lamp.

In blackness one's equilibrium trickles away, and Cribben felt his balance going, and knew to his horror that he was falling straight across that bed. He struck the sheets heavily and paused there in a paralysis of revulsion. Then it came to him that no one lay beneath him.

Revulsion was swallowed in a compelling urgency, and

Cribben slid his hands sweepingly along the covers, in desperate hope of a mistake. But no. There was no form in the bed but his own. Crouching like a great clumsy dog, he hunched against the headboard, while he blinked for any filtered drop of light, show him what it would.

He had left the door ajar, and through the doorway wavered the very dimmest of dim glows, the forlorn hope of the bright sun without. Now that Cribben's eyes had been a little time in the room, he could discern whatever was silhouetted against the doorway—the back of a chair, the edge of the door itself, the knob. And something *moved* into silhouette: imperious nose, pendulous lip, great jaw. So much, before Cribben's heart made its last leaping protest.

WHAT SHADOWS WE PURSUE

"Eleven thousand books," said Mrs. Corr, mildly and factually. In her clear old voice lingered no tone of affection for the vast dusty library, no hint of apprehension of its dignity. "Or nearly eleven thousand. Dr. Corr had Sarah make a card for every one. Why, that's less than thirty cents a volume you're offering, isn't it, Mr. Stoneburner?" With a species of gentle calculation, she let her dim glance slide along the interminable Georgian spines of *A Universal History*. "My . . . but I suppose that's the best we can hope for?"

From thick, faded carpet to moulded-plaster ceiling fifteen feet above, Dr. Corr's books staunchly filled the walls of the long room. Beyond the archway was another room nearly as large, and there books not only jammed the shelves

but lay in heaps upon tables and were monumentally stacked upon the floor. The grand, chill corridor upon which this second room opened also was choked with books, while the shorter hall at right angles, leading from the corridor to what had been Dr. Corr's bedroom, held bound volumes of *The Edinburgh Review* and *Harper's Monthly*. Nor did these comprehend the whole of the collection, for the great skylighted attic, up beyond the graceful curve of the mahogany stair rail, was a storehouse for countless periodicals never bound but neatly tied together in volumes; for obscure governmental reports; for a welter of cheap and damaged editions that Dr. Corr should have sold as waste. But, of course, Dr. Corr never had parted with a book, however wretchedly printed or wretchedly written. He would as soon have sold his daughter—sooner, old Mr. Hanchett said. Hanchett, who had been Stoneburner's cataloguer for five years and cataloguer to other booksellers decades before that, was given to uncharitable judgments. And for all these books, William Stoneburner, bookdealer, now was writing a check.

"Not much more than a quarter each," Stoneburner replied, with his apologetic nod, blowing upon the check. "If you could find a man who wanted the collection for himself, Mrs. Corr, he could give you more than any of us dealers. But who'd have the space for them, in these days? Or the money? Or the leisure to read?" Stoneburner was a little vain of the mien with which he could deliver his genteel and recurrent sigh of *in hoc tempori*. It sat well upon a man who inhabited the valley of the shadow of books, even though he dwelt there as a bourgeois.

"A friend told me," murmured Mrs. Corr, rocking her

little chair softly and inspecting the buttons of her shiny shoes of a fashion forty years obsolete, "that the old Bibles might be worth a great deal, just by themselves. There's a man somewhere who collects old Bibles, this friend said." Despite her having tucked the check into her work basket only this minute, already she was displaying the recriminations so frequently encountered among sellers of books. Stoneburner, knowing the mood, was tolerant.

"I'm sure some people must collect Bibles," he assured the venerable Mrs. Corr in a voice nearly as artless as her own. "Here's what you and I'll do: you can have all the old Bibles. Put them aside and keep them, and sell them to somebody else, if you like. I own too many old Bibles. The price for the library will stand. But I do want to take just one Bible—the Cranmer. I think I know where I can sell that. The rest are yours."

A harsh tone, neither masculine nor feminine, broke in upon this colloquy: the voice of Miss Sarah Corr, who had entered by the door at Stoneburner's back. "What Bible is that, Mr. Stoneburner?" She moved ponderously toward the window seat where a half dozen folio and quarto Bibles clustered, a black dust thick upon their exposed top edges. "You'll get a lot of money for it, I imagine?" She poked unfeelingly the thick book in vellum that Stoneburner indicated.

And Miss Sarah Corr turned her set smile upon Mr. Stoneburner. Larger far than Stoneburner, larger than most men, she was a massive spinster. Fifty? Sixty? Had she ever been young? Not to judge by her dress, which was as timeless as her frail mother's. To be beamed upon by Miss Sarah Corr was not altogether pleasant. When Stoneburner first had seen that broad smile, he had been standing upon the steps of the austere stone house of Dr. Corr, a house somber even on an Indian-summer evening; and Miss Corr had opened to his ring with some caution, and then had said, with that peculiar smile, "You're the gentlemen who buys books? The one with the advertisement in the telephone directory?"

A month gone, that evening. The month had been a time of delicate negotiation with Mrs. Corr and Miss Corr, two recluses mightily ignorant of the contents of these eleven thousand volumes, mightily afraid of losing a fortune. It was a good library, but there was no fortune in it: the library of a man who read, not of a man who collected.

"It's going to bring me sixty or seventy dollars, Miss Corr," Stoneburner told her, unruffled. "Only that for a Cranmer Bible. On all these shelves, perhaps there are six or eight books people will pay that much for. The rest—why, they're good books, the kind of books Dr. Corr read. I think I'd have liked to know Dr. Corr."

"Yes, yes?" sighed Mrs. Corr, civilly, still rocking. She accepted Stoneburner's remark as a conventional compliment, apparently, and volunteered no comment upon her husband. Her *late* husband, Stoneburner had thought when initially he browsed through this house; but while the Corr women spoke of the doctor as one forever gone, they never seemed quite to use the past tense. So Stoneburner had inquired of old Hanchett, who knew something of every man within this century that had bought very many books in the city.

"Dr. Corr is one of those chaps that wither up and the wind blows away," old Hanchett had said, being himself invincibly portly and rubicund. "Haven't seen him in several years. He let his friends go because he liked the books better, and he came out into the light less and less . . . Well, you've seen his wife and daughter. Books cost; the Corr women had to manage with one new dress a year, or every other year. And then they gave up their card-parties. As time went on, Corr decided that his women's mission in life was to make catalogue cards for his books and to do a bit of dusting. He used to take his wife for an hour's walk after supper; then back to his library, and she to her parlor to sew, until it was time for sleep—Corr to his bedroom (books helter-skelter on the floor), she to hers.

"The daughter? Oh, the girl was queer to begin with. You'll see it, Mr. Stoneburner: she has her little ways. Maybe she was one of the things that drove Corr away from people, into books. Corr was allergic—allergic to people. Ah, but books, though . . . I'll hand it to him there. No, it's been years since I had a word with him. As he dried up, even the evening walk got to be too long a vacation from his books. I wonder if he has books where he is now? I don't know exactly when they took him away, but Mrs. Corr told my cousin that they sent him out West for his health. They don't seem to expect him back. His *health*, eh?" Here Hanchett had tapped a plump finger against his forehead, uncharitably. "One-way ticket, Mr. Stoneburner. And is the money nearly gone now, too? I suppose it costs to keep the doctor in the West for his *health*. Why, the doctor would be a screaming devil if he knew the library was being sold. He was a tall, white husk of a man, decent-spoken, a gold mine for the dealers."

Still Mrs. Corr rocked, soothing away this reference of

Stoneburner's to her husband as she and her daughter were wont to pass over such comments—nothing of pride in their manner, nothing of resentment. "Yes, yes? Well, now—the house will seem almost empty with the books gone, won't it? All sorts of people are looking for places to live these days, I hear. I suppose we could rent part of this great big house of ours. But who would want to live here? It's too dirty." And Mrs. Corr laughed her delicate little laugh, and Miss Corr added her deep chuckle.

Candid, this. The Corrs were not deficient in a certain withered wit. Undoubtedly the Corr house was too dirty for anyone but the Corrs. From the parlor ceiling, the paper hung down in festoons that obscured the gilt-framed paintings on the walls. Plaster was falling in the attic, for the roof has begun to leak in Dr. Corr's time. One suspected that Dr. Corr's allergy toward humanity extended even to roofers and plumbers and paperers. Certain utilitarian improvements had been installed in his house only with extreme tardiness: the lighting, for instance. Apparently possessed of a reactionary confidence that the days of high old Roman virtue would return, Dr. Corr had cherished three systems of illumination, each ready to function in a pinch. Candelabra and kerosene lamps were to be seen, tarnished and topsy-turvy, in this corner or that; gas jets still protruded from plaster or panelling, and could be lit; but the actual artificial light came from naked bulbs dangling like hanged felons from the ceilings—many of them the early bamboo filament sort that terminate in a glassy spike, since the Corrs lived in three or four rooms and turned on these other switches scarcely more than twice in a month.

Not a practical man, Dr. Corr; nor was Mrs. Corr a practical woman; yet she seemed to have a canny eye for a dollar, possibly out of necessity. Her rocking uninterrupted, she continued, "Now, Mr. Stoneburner, I don't suppose you mean the books in the attic are included, do you? Those still belong to us?"

Stoneburner certainly had thought they were his. All the same, they were trash, except for the periodicals, which needed binding. And it was unpleasant to deny a crumb of victory to an impractical lady in her eighties. He was about to say, "You're quite welcome to them," when Mr. Markashian entered. Mr. Markashian had overheard something of the conversation. Mr. Markashian had a habit of overhearing, Stoneburner reflected.

"Of course they belong to us, Mother," pronounced Markashian, with emphasis.

Mrs. Corr obviously was not Markashian's mother, for he was a Levantine; despite the Armenian name, he had more the look of an Anatolian Greek. He was her son-in-law, nevertheless, a public accountant from Newark, firm in a decided opinion that he knew the world, and deserved well of it. "Markashian never dared turn up while the doctor was in the house," Hanchett had told Stoneburner. "He married Lilly Corr on the sly. Both of them got cheated."

But the vanishing of the doctor from the scene and the scent of a sale of family assets had drawn the worldly Mr. Markashian from his accustomed pursuits in New Jersey. He left his wife behind to tend the children, informing her that family honor and prosperity now were his responsibility. As a man of business, Mrs. Corr and Miss Sarah Corr appeared to reverence him unwillingly; but it was clear to Stoneburner that Markashian did not want the books to be sold at all, preferring the chance of inheriting the library to the chance of inheriting a remnant of the cash. As a man of business and as a simple man, Stoneburner loathed Markashian, who rejoiced in the best suits and the worst manners Stoneburner had observed for some years.

"You understand that, don't you?" went on Markashian, turning to Stoneburner. "The books in the attic don't go with the others. There's highly valuable property upstairs."

"What money you can extract from the books in the attic," Stoneburner told him sourly, "I make you a present of."

"That's settled, then," grinned Markashian, on a note of triumph. "What's the book you're holding, Sarah?"

Miss Sarah Corr gave Markashian one of her long stares, and then a long smile, and suddenly came out with, "An old Bible worth thirty dollars. Mr. Stoneburner wants this one." A single bond of sympathy joined Stoneburner and Miss Corr: distrust of Markashian.

"What, this lovely old ancestral Bible?" groaned Markashian. "An heirloom! Gutenburg Bible, isn't it? It mustn't leave the family."

"It's not a Gutenburg, I'm sorry to inform you, Mr. Markashian; and it's my property. I can't have more books extracted from my purchase. Would you prefer to return the check to me, Mrs. Corr?" He extended his hand toward her. Though a cheery little man, Stoneburner was capable of firmness.

Patting her work basket in alarm, Mrs. Corr declared she had no intention of breaking the bargain. "Everything but the other Bibles, and the books in the attic, and the few things Mr. Markashian took for himself yesterday after you left—everything else is yours, Mr. Stoneburner. My, what a strange house this will be with the books gone! You'll take them all out yourself, Mr. Stoneburner? You won't bring anyone to help? We'd rather carry them for you ourselves than have strangers running upstairs."

This was a matter of consequence with her and with Sarah Corr, who turned her stagnant look on him. The intensity of the appeal somewhat embarrassed Stoneburner and seemed to surprise even Markashian. But Stoneburner already had agreed to the stipulation. It was natural enough: dirty though they confessed their house to be, still they hardly would want it inspected by chance comers.

"All eleven thousand, Mrs. Corr—I'll lug them to the truck myself. I'll need a whole week, off and on. We'll have to take care with some of the folios: they're shaky. Heavy things, books—I'll be stiff when it's done. Will it suit you if I start at nine tomorrow morning?"

Sarah Corr went with him to the double-bolted front door, through the vaulted corridor where two walnut clocks ticked alternately amid the ashes of magnificence, and she let him out into the night. He swung away from that ponderous, ever-beaming face, with the close-cropped grey hair that turned it almost masculine. "You've seen the attic," she said. "You won't need to go there again, after tonight?"

"Since those books aren't mine, no."

"That's nice of you," Miss Corr concluded, closing the door in his face. He listened to her bolt it, hesitating for a moment on the steps. As he loitered, it occurred to him that he had not heard Sarah Corr's slow stride back through the corridor. She must be standing just inside the door, to make sure he was gone. Shrugging, Stoneburner went.

A light covered truck especially equipped with wooden racks was the property of Stoneburner's Bookshop. And this Stoneburner parked close by the porch of the Corr house next morning, ready to commence moving one tier of the books in the library proper. Greeting him with her invariable hesitant commendation of the weather, Mrs. Corr admitted him. She wore that black dress which hid her ankles—a dowdy figure, but not vulgar. Back into her parlor she tottered, and Stoneburner went his quiet way up the circling stairs to the library. As he trod the stair carpet, he heard feet hastily descending from a higher level—the attic, of course; and he took them for Mr. Markashian's feet. But when he reached the library floor, nothing was to be seen of Markashian. Perhaps he had ducked into one of the chilly bedrooms off the corridor. Markashian was given to judicious ducking.

Methodically dusting the top of each volume with a piece of flannel, Stoneburner took the books from a tier of shelves close to the window and stacked them in tidy heaps convenient for carrying downstairs. A gap appeared upon one of the shelves. The morning before, a set of Bacon had reposed there, and Stoneburner assumed it was part of his purchase. But finding it gone in the afternoon, he had inquired of Mrs. Corr, to be told that "Mr. Markashian thought it ought to be his—useful in his work." Stoneburner had waived the matter.

A decrepit little ladder enabled Stoneburner to reach the higher shelves; he balanced upon it, dusting. In this volume or that, Dr. Corr had inserted neat slips of paper to mark favorite passages; small checks in the margins pointed to some mighty line or kernel of wit. Himself a leisurely man, Stoneburner now and then opened a book to glance at these passages, and generally was much taken with the doctor's choice. He began to form an image of Dr. Corr other than the "sneer of cold command" that Hanchett's description had left in his mind. A solitary man, this Dr. Corr; but then, how could he be other than alien to his mousy wife and queer daughter and infuriating son-in-law? Indeed, Stoneburner experienced the beginnings of awe for a noble mind in provincial obscurity. Corr's family may have paid back his disdain in that ferocious envy the vulgar feel toward the proud. Bound to them he may have been; but until now they had been his slaves.

Stoneburner took down Fuller's *The Holy State and the Profane State*—a fine glossy seventeenth-century binding. "Cesare Borgia, His Life," Corr had underlined in the index, and had marked the page by inserting a note-card. The bookseller ran his eye along the passages checked: "The throne and the bed cannot severally abide partners. . . ." "For he could neither lengthen the land nor lessen the sea in Italie. . . ." "He preferred the state of his body to the body of his state." Why, even a touch of fun in this Dr. Corr. Stoneburner put the quarto upon his dusted stack; and, having done with this shelf, glanced at the books on the window seat There was a gap among them.

What sort of fool did they think him? For the Cranmer Bible was gone. He was inured to pilferage and aware that the average person with whom he dealt thought a single volume could hardly be missed among so many. But in the present instance, Stoneburner had specifically claimed the Cranmer for his own the previous day, and it was too bulky and too valuable for them to suppose he would forget it wholly. This was more than Stoneburner was disposed to endure. Though angry, he was self-possessed, and he turned to face the room, wondering if they could have tucked the book into some drawer. They would not dare hide it absolutely, since that was theft; more probably they would endeavor to lose it in some pile of trash, trusting he might pass it by. And so he recalled the steps he had heard briskly descending from the attic when, an hour before, he had entered the house.

Mrs. Corr was downstairs, and Sarah Corr with her, no doubt; Markashian—for surely it was he who had scuttled from the attic—would not be inclined to face him at this moment, even supposing him only across the corridor. A quiet survey of the attic could do no harm.

Stoneburner walked into the corridor and turned up the spiralling stair. At the top the door stood ajar. Standing on the last step and resting his arm upon the balustrade, Stoneburner sent an exploratory glance within. One enormous room, this attic, into which the sun penetrated dully through a cupola skylight. Sundry boxes and articles of old furniture were scattered about the center of the floor, but Dr. Corr had kept the place fairly clear of rubbish so that he could get to his shelves of magazines along the walls. Right opposite the door, in line with Stoneburner's eyes, was a broad tier of worthless novels, no doubt bought by Dr. Corr with other books at some auction.

These novels had been disturbed. Six or seven had fallen to the floor, and another gap indicated that more had tumbled from the shelves. Had Markashian been sliding the

Cranmer among this trash and been interrupted at his game? Stoneburner raised one foot to the final step of the staircase.

But he was prevented. Sharp and resistless, a grip pinned his arm against the balustrade. Half a second he paused to quiet his leaping nerves, and then looked round to see Miss Sarah Corr at his back, her great hand clamped upon his wrist, her face set in that inimitable smile. The smile grew broader. As it spread, her fingers dug into his wrist as if to find a passage through. She must have tiptoed painstakingly after him, weasel behind goose. And in her face there was no more of mercy than of sanity.

"Sarah!" whispered Mrs. Corr from the foot of the staircase, and commenced laboriously to climb toward them. At that soft cry, Miss Sarah Corr relaxed her clutch, and the smile sank into something nearer humanity, but still she did not speak.

Mrs. Corr ascended the infinite way to their side, and said to him, most politely and casually, "Did you need something in the attic, Mr. Stoneburner?" Her old eyes cried out some awful disturbance. But what?

"Someone seems to have been looking over the Cranmer Bible," Stoneburner answered, something of a quaver in his voice. "Do you suppose it might have been left up here by mistake?"

Embarrassment he had expected, perhaps shamed denial; but not this assuagement that came into the faces of the Corr women. "Oh, I'm sorry you have the trouble of looking for it," said Mrs. Corr with a tiny sigh. "Sarah and I will see if we can help." And together they entered the attic.

To the left of the cupola skylight stood an imposing oak desk, a pile of old ledgers sprawled upon it. Stoneburner had noticed it before. But now the capacious drawers were pulled open, and bundles of letters and papers and photographs tossed out of them and spread in confusion beside the ledgers. Sarah Corr drew a heavy breath, and Mrs. Corr glanced round the big room, and then they went at the desk with a sort of horror-struck frenzy. Markashian's curiosity and covetousness extended beyond the library purchase to the property of his mother-in-law and sister-in-law, Stoneburner surmised; and doubtless his coming had interrupted Mr. Markashian's prowling. As mother and daughter packed papers into drawers and cubby-holes with a gingerly haste, Stoneburner examined a photograph of a white-haired, hollow-cheeked man in a high collar that lay face upward. "Oh, Dr. Corr?" he inquired. "And these are his papers? A fine face."

They stopped sorting the papers, and, wordless, looked at him. Sarah Corr raised a massive hand, and for a foolish moment he thought she meant to strike him; but instead she laid a finger upon her lips. Then she took the picture from his hand, turning it downward in the act, and laid it at the bottom of a drawer. This silence was contagious. Quite dumb, he stood by while they cleared away the confusion and shut the violated drawers and padded back toward the stairs. Then—"Ah, there's the Bible," said Stoneburner, seeing the quarto among a heap of the fallen novels and bending to retrieve it.

"My . . . Mr. Markashian must have been reading it," murmured Mrs. Corr, touching his coat sleeve—almost tugging at him. As he rose with the Bible, he noticed a deep, an incalculably deep, space behind the gap from which the novels had tumbled.

"Why, what's happened here, Mrs. Corr? Have you lost some books down a hole?" He glanced into it. A hole, yes; a very great hole. A stair well, with steps descending into a black abyss. This tier of shelves veiled, and sealed away, was some disused back way into the attic. When he leaned forward for a closer look, his shoulder brushed against a tottering novel, and that book, too, fell backward from its place, bounding four or five steps into the filthy gloom and then flopping to its rest upon the last visible tread.

"You! Don't you dare!" The stifled scream had come from Sarah Corr—the most nearly feminine expression he had heard from her. Her teeth were gritted, but she seemed beyond smiling. Mrs. Corr ran a hand along her daughter's arm.

"Those are the old stairs for the maids, Mr. Stoneburner," Mrs. Corr explained, looking not at him but at the gap in the shelves. "They've been boarded since I don't know when. That's one reason we hoped you wouldn't need the books up here: the stairs would seem so odd without books to hide them.

"I'm glad the Bible wasn't lost. Do you need us to help you dust downstairs?" She took his arm; he helped her down the staircase, Sarah closing the door tightly behind them. There was no key in it, and Stoneburner suspected that nearly every key in the house had been mislaid years before.

In the library, with the Corr women gone down to the parlor, Stoneburner placed his resurrected Bible among the dusted books and went on with his stacking. A pox upon the book-ignorant folk who think every dog-eared Victorian New Testament a collector's treasure beyond the dreams of avarice! How often had he heard over his telephone some hesitant voice inquiring, "Do you buy old books? Really old books? What do you pay? I've got a *really* old Bible here. Authorized Version. London, *1884* . . ."

All too strong was this spirit in that nervous pair, the Corr women. Possibly, though, they were endowed with redeeming virtues. They had seemed genuinely shocked at Markashian's profanation of the doctor's papers, presumably left undisturbed, out of sentiment, ever since that gaunt shell of learning was sent somewhere into the West to linger out the little time still vouchsafed his wreck.

Now Stoneburner began taking down the volumes of a good set of Burke, their pages much marked and checked in the doctor's hand. Such pencillings impair the value of second-hand books; but since Stoneburner read books as well as sold them, he did not complain overmuch. What sort of thing had Corr favored in Burke? Opening at random, he found a sentence doubly underlined: "What shadows we are, and what shadows we pursue."

Just so, old doctor. And true for bookworms like you and me, most especially—thus Stoneburner to himself. You even more than I, thank God. He put the volume with the others and stretched his tired arms. As he rested, a noise of voices full of anger drifted faintly to him from the parlor below. Well, had the Corr women had enough of that reluctantly-revered Setebos of a son-in-law, that dandy with the vulturine profile and the flaccid hand? The temptation to eavesdrop was overwhelming. Stoneburner bent over the stair well, where the words could be made out sufficiently.

". . . Only to look for the receipts, Mother." Yes, it was Markashian, half the cocksureness gone out of his tones, a Markashian taken aback at such vehemence over a bout of snooping.

Sarah Corr was answering him, or rather drowning him out. "Meddling, meddling, stirring things up! What do you want to poke into? What do you want to bring on us? Take your pictures, take your books, but don't poke. Take your money, but don't pry! No more sense . . ."

Markashian's reply was not wholly audible, but Stoneburner made out something about "no harm" and "a thousand miles away." Miss Corr roared down the oily voice again, her mother's low entreaty interrupting her. Then a door was shut and Stoneburner was prevented from hearing the rest; but this he caught before the colloquy was suppressed: "He always slept light, and he knew what you were after, and he could get into your dreams, and now he'll stir, the devil! That old, white, sneering, creepy devil! That's what!"

Was it the absent Dr. Corr thus described by his daughter? A nice family, a cordial household. Well, time for lunch, Stoneburner realized. He skipped down the stairs and tapped at the parlor door and glanced within. The three were standing in the middle of the faded room, all taut at his knock. "Back at two, if that's all right," Stoneburner told them, and went his way. Yes, a jolly family.

* * *

The grimmest of all aspects of the book trade is the carrying of big volumes upstairs or down; and just this was to be Stoneburner's afternoon task. Commencing at two, he kept at it faithfully for more than an hour. The Corrs and Markashian stayed out of his way, withdrawn in their parlor with its dingy plush chairs. As Stoneburner lugged perhaps the fortieth stack of volumes toward the front door, there came a crash above. Had the books piled in the library fallen? Hardly. He had arranged them neatly, and the noise seemed more distant. From the parlor peered Markashian and Mrs. Corr.

"Perhaps some magazines in the attic toppled," Stoneburner offered.

"My, no," said Mrs. Corr, almost inaudibly, holding tight to the door-jamb. Markashian went up the stairs; Mrs. Corr opened her mouth as if to call after him, but no words followed. So remarkable was the look she sent up the stair well that Stoneburner waited for Markashian's report.

He came down with his accustomed strut. "Three shelves in the attic tipped over somehow," Markashian informed them. "Sarah ought to pick them up before long—some of the shelves in front of the closed-off stairs."

Without a word, Mrs. Corr vanished back into the parlor, and Stoneburner went on with his load. But as he closed the house door, he heard from the parlor what sounded like an hysterical gurgle; and also it sounded like Sarah Corr.

When five o'clock was chimed by the two clocks in the hall, Stoneburner still was lugging books to his truck. For a moment's rest, he seated himself in a rickety chair amid his dusted stacks and leafed through the first collected edition of Harrington, *Oceana* Harrington. "Dr. Randolph Corr," with a flourish, was written upon the flyleaf. "Purchased in Bristol, April 23, 1912." Ah, how everything passes! The doctor had spent his life amassing these dead men's fancies, and here strove the undoer of the great library, dispersing in some days what Corr had built in as many decades. Perhaps it was as well that he had not known the doctor, Stoneburner reflected: had he ever seen Corr, this work of destruction might have weighed upon his conscience. One man's pleasure, another's agony. . . . He lifted another stack, cradled it in his arms, and proceeded carefully downstairs.

Halfway down, an odor drifted round him. Undeniable— yes, gas. Stoneburner took the books to the stair foot and then tapped at the parlor.

"Who?" It was Mrs. Corr's voice, with a quaver. He entered. Mrs. Corr and Sarah Corr sat near to each other in two armchairs that faced the door. Markashian was not there. They looked at him with disturbing intensity.

"Could you have forgotten to turn off the kitchen range, Miss Corr? I smell gas somewhere."

"Gas, gas, gas," repeated Sarah Corr, with a heave of her heavy body; but she did not rise, nor did her mother. Truly, Miss Corr had her ways.

A pregnant pause; then, from Mrs. Corr, "Mr. Markashian is out. Might I ask you, Mr. Stoneburner, to see if the gas is turned on?"

Still they did not rise nor offer to assist, nor even to come so far as the door with him. And they watched him as he went into the corridor.

No, it was not the kitchen range. Now that he was on the ground floor, it seemed to Stoneburner that the faint gas-odor drifted to him from above. And when he was on the library floor, it came stronger still; and he thought it must emanate from the attic. Up the stair. As evening approached, the attic grew unpleasantly dark. Those books still lay tumbled from the shelves before the sealed staircase. Yes, the odor was most strong in this dim room. Three gas brackets in the attic: the first two securely turned off—indeed, screwed tight so firmly that he could not budge them with his bare hands. But the third was open, the gas pouring from it. Closing the jet, Stoneburner reflected upon his good fortune not to have been smoking. Had Markashian turned on a light while up here, blown it out, and forgotten to twist the little knob below the mantle? A man unfamiliar with gas mantles might well blunder. But why hadn't Markashian switched on the single electric bulb dangling near the skylight? A most eccentric ménage.

"Ah!" cried Stoneburner. And then, "Who is it?" For two or three books had fallen suddenly, an earthquake in this attic silence. He jerked about; but there was no one, and surely there could have been no whisper. Yes, more books had dropped inward from those shelves before the dead-end staircase. He reached into that hole back of the novels to retrieve whatever volumes had escaped downward. But they had tumbled beyond his reach—he could make them out, vaguely, a half-dozen steps down, one flopped open on its spine, its pages slowly slipping from left to right as if turned by fingers indiscernible.

"By God, no!" muttered Stoneburner, low.

For no one could have whispered to him, whispered ever so slyly and incoherently, out of the abyss. Stoneburner shrugged uneasily, dusted off his trouser-knees, and fixed his mind resolutely upon book-prices current.

He trotted down to the library then, picked up his Cranmer Bible to ensure it against another misadventure, and proceeded to the ground-floor corridor. The Corr women still sat immobile in those lumpy chairs.

"Someone didn't close the jet in the attic, but it's all right now. I think I'll go to dinner. Will it inconvenience you people if I finish moving the section I'm on about seven o'clock or so?"

Sarah Corr had worn that smile so literally mordant, but without warning she said fiercely, "Old devil! Old, white, creepy devil!"

Was it extreme old age or a genuine power of dissimulation that enabled Mrs. Corr so placidly to gloss over her daughter's outbursts? At any rate, she nodded politely to Stoneburner. "We'll be glad to have you back this evening." But ah, her eyes. And she did not accompany him to the porch. So Stoneburner left them in the moldy, tattered parlor.

* * *

Nearer eight o'clock than seven, Stoneburner pulled the tarnished bell-knob at Dr. Corr's house. No clang responded within, so far as he could tell; but he always had suspected that the bell did not work, and that Miss Corr had known of his presence only because she had been peering from some window. He knocked, and knocked again. No one came. And now he observed that the whole house was a darker mass of blackness against the night—not one window lit. Had the Corrs gone out? Too early for bed, surely. He tried the door: not locked, fortunately. Closing it behind him, Stoneburner felt for a light switch, and could find none; everything in the Corr house was tucked out of sight.

Ah, well, he knew the stairs and could find the light in the library. Inside the library doorway his fingers encountered the switch, and the old-fashioned bulb sent its radiance into the corridor. And then, as he was about to cross the threshold into the sea of books, out of the corner of his eye he perceived something unfamiliar, something inappropriate, protruding between two posts of the stair rail to the attic. A chill went through him. For the unfamiliar thing was a flabby hand. Behind it? Whoever was behind it must be lying prone on the dark stairs. A quick-witted little man, Stoneburner thought of the miniature flashlight attached to his key-ring. Pulling it from his coat, he stepped to the stairs and sent the beam upward.

Markashian: nothing worse. Mr. Markashian lay with his unconscious face slanting downward, as if he had tripped and fallen—and the blood on one olive cheek seemed to confirm this. A closer look suggested that he was breathing, though thoroughly stunned. Kneeling in the dark by the accountant, Stoneburner listened for any step or rustle. But surely nothing moved within the house, and its stone walls barred the noise of the street. Mrs. Corr and Sarah Corr? Somehow Stoneburner dared not call out. He left Markashian, and slipped with infinite care down the carpeted treads to the ground floor, every hint of a creak from the old boards an agony to his nerves, his own faint shadow on the papered wall a hunched menace.

Hesitating at the parlor door, he still could detect no sound. None? Why, perhaps the gentlest of sounds, not a hiss, not a swish, but the suggestion of a breath of air. Stoneburner did not desire to turn that knob.

All the same, he turned it, and pushed open the door, and

was met by a wave of gas, long pent within. Holding his breath, he fumbled for the light-switch. This time, luck being with him, the light came on. Mrs. Corr still sat in her chair, but Sarah Corr had slumped out of hers upon the rug. Their faces were toward him, unmistakably dead, faces with such a look as drifts through dreams.

* * *

Several curious and unpleasant matters concerning Mr. Markashian's past were known to the police captain who arrived at Dr. Corr's house ten minutes after Stoneburner's call. No one could doubt that Markashian had been quite as odd, on occasion, as had been his connections by marriage, nor that his mind was seriously impaired at present, nor that his case required not a trial, but committal to an asylum. At least, none could doubt these conclusions but Stoneburner, and he only confusedly. Why Mrs. Corr and Miss Corr had not risen from their chairs to shut off the jets remained unexplained, unless it was from terror of Markashian.

After two hours in the echoing house, the police discovered at the foot of the disused maids' stairs what remained of the doctor—Dr. Corr, who had gone West only figuratively, his body having been crammed into a closet, or large cupboard, in that sealed passage. Within the cupboard was a gas mantle, and the police captain speculated that the old man, still living, had been bound, pushed into the closet, and left for some hours with the gas turned on. He must have been a vigorous old man, Dr. Corr: great strength would have been required to subdue him. Passed from this life for many months, and that by what must have been an act of explosive violence, Corr bore the expression of a domestic hatred that had smouldered many a year. Markashian, rallying, disclaimed any knowledge of the doctor's death. And so far, but no further, the police believed him.

The police put the livid Markashian on a sofa in what had been the doctor's office. After a time—he watching the closed door intently all the while—Markashian defiantly informed them (his slippery vanity somewhat reviving) that he had gone to the attic to rummage the doctor's desk for a will. "My wife has her rights, after all"—and Dr. Corr, presumably never to return from the West, might have left behind a testament of sorts. Stoneburner watched that vulturine bravado pale and sag then; but Markashian went on, stumblingly, to say that he had run downstairs and had fallen, and knew nothing of what followed in the Corr house.

"Why did you hurry on the stairs?" the police captain demanded.

"Because it was coming up, up from behind the books," Markashian cried out, gripping the sofa arm.

"What do you mean?" The captain was infected with this man's dread.

"Oh, it woke. The books falling, the mouth, the long hair, the dusty hands!" That said, Markashian sank sobbing to the floor. From the rim of one high shelf, past the leather spines of fine bindings which gleamed from their cases, a streamer of soot floated downward to settle upon his cheek.

LOST LAKE

🔔

A fatality clings to some places: not merely to historic houses or to battlefields, but to obscure corners recorded only in the short and simple annals of the poor. One such place—almost at the back of my old house in Mecosta, Michigan—is Lost Lake, with the derelict fields and neglected woods round it. The genius loci is malevolent.

Lost Lake is a dark little sheet of water perhaps twice the size of Walden Pond. Closely shut in by maples, oaks, birches, and pines, probably it looks rather as Walden Pond looked in Thoreau's day; but it has no philosopher-hermit, and none is likely to settle there now. Indeed, no one is quite sure who owns it: the title to most of its shore seems to be in the hands of an old lady who lives in a fashionable suburb of Detroit, but she never visits the place and does not answer letters.

It lies about two miles down a twisting sand road at the back of our decayed village of Mecosta, which had two thousand residents in my great-grandfather's day and has sunk to two hundred now. I am very fond of the lonely and labyrinthine walk from my house to Lost Lake, through the sand and sumac and Indian paintbrush and scrub oaks. But one disconcerting fact seems to be whispered over the face of the water, out of the lily pads and up from the butt ends of logs never salvaged by the old lumbermen: no one who tries to live beside Lost Lake lives very long. It is fatal even to cattle, for in the old days many went down to death in its quicksand bottom, which is very deep.

Spring-fed, cold, and black, the lake has no regular outlet, though perhaps at the height of the April rains some water makes its way over the sand lip that rings Lost Lake round and trickles down through masses of Indian pipe and huckleberry bushes and rotten trunks to a branch of the Little Muskegon. No boats are kept there, and few holes are chopped through the thick ice in winter—for fish seem to be nearly as scarce as people at Lost Lake.

Moribund village and dead lake are set in a stretch of sandy and glaciated land that has vanquished American optimism. We are less than two hundred miles by road from Detroit, and only some sixty-five from the furniture factories of Grand Rapids. But if you draw a line westward across the southern peninsula of Michigan, roughly from Saginaw Bay to Muskegon, north of that line you will find, except for economic islands of manufacturing or decent land, a sparse population, dry summers, cold winters, and rural poverty. This is the cut-over land, the stump country, deforested seventy or eighty years ago and only in recent years beginning to regain its cover of good-sized trees. Some of it ought never to have been plowed. At a time when the American population has swelled to bursting in much of the country, the Upper Peninsula and the northern half of the Lower Peninsula of Michigan have experienced a depopulation like that of the Scottish highlands.

Though near the southern limit of this stump country, Mecosta is an impoverished and forgotten village, set in a township that has only two real farms still cultivated. A mile-long stretch of wide street, faced with false-fronted white frame buildings as in a Western movie set: that is Mecosta. There are more gaps than buildings along the street nowadays, and our biggest store burned recently. A great cedar swamp, sixteen miles long, stretched up the little river that divides the village into "Downtown" and "The Hill"; the deer herd there in winter, and some bears live at the heart of Hughes' Swamp. Thick wood lots of mingled pine and hardwoods, nearly thirty glacial lakes, scattered little homesteads of twenty or forty or eighty acres, and a vast overgrown upland expanse we call "Skyberia" lie round about Mecosta. Log cabins and tarpaper shacks dot this infertile township and its neighbors; subsistence farming aside, the only money crops are cucumbers and beans. Living here is inexpensive and leisurely, but there is no work for the rising generation. The country is nearly as naked as Connaught, but not so green.

Not many centuries ago, all this land must have been tundra; then the first forest slowly grew, and some few Pottawattomie and Chippewa and Ottawa and Ojibway Indians came to live among the trees. Mecosta, named after the Pottawattomie chief who ceded the land to the whites, means "Little Cub Bear." Sometimes we think that old Mecosta got the better of whatever bargain he made with our ancestors, for the land is blow sand with a precarious inch or two of humus deposited upon it. Only three or four Indians still live roundabout, and those are assimilated to the ways of their white or colored neighbors, for the last basket-weavers died unnoticed in their swamp near Pretty Lake some years since.

An Indian strain survives, nevertheless, in some of the colored and white families. Our Negro population is older than our white population: for several families of escaped or emancipated slaves (most of them having taken refuge in Ontario during the fifties and sixties) came here in Conestoga wagons at the end of the Civil War, settling down peaceably beside the Indians. An old colored community like this, with its own church, its own leading families, and its own traditions (recorded, a good many of them, in my friend Richard Dorson's book *Michigan Negro Folklore*) is a rarity in Michigan. Most of our "colored" people are very light skinned now. Every summer they celebrate Old Settlers' Day (a euphemism for Emancipation Day), their kinfolk who have settled in Detroit or Chicago or Grand Rapids or Lansing coming back to the site of the first Negro farm, by Schoolsection Lake, for a picnic and a dance.

Rhineland Catholics had begun to clear farms near Mecosta a few years before the colored people came, although their village center was the now-vanished Bingen Post Office. About half the population of our township and the neighboring districts is Catholic now, most of them of German descent, with an Irish infusion.

But as for Mecosta proper, it was the virgin forest that

brought the white people in the seventies and eighties, many of these New York lumbermen from the Finger Lakes. My great-grandfather Amos Johnson and his uncle were among them, and also my great-grandfather Isaac Pierce, who had been to the California gold rush. They strode into this country and swept off a great part of the forest; and, the better trees gone, most of them marched on to the Pacific coast.

The Panic of '93 struck a dreadful blow at this land. My great-grandfather's bank failed, other bankers round about shot themselves, and most of the remaining timber was cut and sold for what little the market could pay. My great-grandfather and some of the other New Yorkers held on grimly, but Mecosta never knew flush times after '93. Other racial stocks have appeared in this century, among them Polish and Ukrainian dirt farmers, and in summer the fields and the broad street of the village are full of Mexican and Puerto Rican farm laborers. An odd population and an odd country.

From the tall windows of my angular old white bracketed house on The Hill—called by the less reverent denizens of the Downtown back in the saloon days, I fear in mockery, Piety Hill—I look out on three sides to the woods, creeping back over the decayed little farms. (As the farmers diminish in number, so do the prairie chickens, a dying breed when the forest reclaims their feeding grounds.) First come the poplars and the birches, and presently the pines, and the maples and oaks and elms. One thing we have in plenty—firewood. Some twenty or thirty acres of giant hemlocks remain in one of the swamps, the last of the forest primeval.

Until quite recently, Mecosta had its reputed witches,

mighty cursers of milking cows. A certain glamour, in its root, non-Hollywood sense, has spread over this barren land from its first settlement. Just down one road, in a tar-paper shack covered with roses, a kerosene lamp was kept burning all night to keep off the ha'nts, according to my great-aunts. In the early years of white settlement, the Spiritualists and Swedenborgians were strong in Mecosta; a Spiritualist church with a tall white steeple overlooked the village; and my family, like the James family, were in the thick of that uncanny business. On my bookshelves, my great-grandfather's black set of Swedenborg's works stands cheek by jowl with his set of Macaulay's *History*.

This old house of mine, thought by some people, including myself, to be haunted, has known its séances and sepulchral voices and table-levitations. Once an odd affair took place in the front parlor. My great-grandfather's uncle, Giles Gilbert, was the lumber baron of these parts; and his nephews were with him in the trade. One of them, my great-grandfather Amos Johnson's younger brother, went round every Saturday night through the woods to pay the wages of the rough crews in the lumber camps, the cash in a bag, a pistol in his pocket. One Saturday night he did not return; and though they searched for him the next day, there was no trace. Then a séance was held in our parlor, the shutters closed and the lamps extinguished; my great-grandfather, a massive red-bearded man, sitting at the head of the table in silence. Presently, out of the dark, Amos Johnson murmured, "I see him"; and he described his brother as lying face down in an opening in a particular part of the forest. They went to that opening, and there his brother was, shot through the head, the money gone. It was a rough country then, and retains its mysteries still.

If one knocks at the door of some remote farmhouse in the dead of night, even nowadays, one may get no answer, or may hear a gun bolt being driven home—and nothing more. I know, having sought assistance on lonely roads at the witching hour. Also, in my magisterial capacity as justice of the peace, I have come upon some remarkable eccentrics and curious occurrences.

* * *

So the fatality that clings to Lost Lake is no great subject for wonder in this stump country. It is only that the genius loci is a trifle more somber at Lost Lake.

You go down to Lost Lake along a faint track that twists through plantations of pine and spruce. If you should take, at a fork, what appears to be the better path, you would end foundered in a wonderful huckleberry marsh. You choose the fainter trail, then—it is easy to miss, and I have got myself lost more than once on these ghosts of roads—and wander over the barrens until Lost Lake is reached. Even then, you may pass by the pond without seeing it, for the woods lie dense all round. The odds are that you will have this lake to yourself: a pleasant lonely spot, with its little animals and ducks and perhaps a loon, but brooding.

Close to the eastern shore of the lake, in a sun-stricken clearing, remain the foundations of a house. Here George Washington, one of the Old Settler Negroes, established his homestead and endeavored to farm these sandy acres. In one way or another, his neighbors took parts of his land away from him; he grew old and poor and lived quite alone.

On a summer day, some kinfolk came to visit him; they

knocked, but were not answered. When they forced open the door, they found George Washington lying stiff and stark in his bunk, apparently starved and worked to death. That night they sat by the corpse, planning to bury him the following day. But after midnight the dead man rose precipitately from under the sheet. His kinfolk fled screeching down the sand road, and did not venture back until the next day. They found him out hoeing; he had got over his fit. Not until January did they return to visit him, and on that visit, too, they got no answer to their knocking. They went in, on that hard winter day, and found George Washington stiff as before, and this time indubitably dead. Taken sick, he had dragged into his house what logs and branches he could gather close by, and had gone to bed, keeping up the fire by thrusting logs into the open mouth of the stove and pushing them further in as they burned. When the last log was consumed, George Washington froze.

The Washington farm was taken by a man who intended to raise potatoes. He bought quantities of seed-potatoes and of Paris green, to combat the potato-bugs. But the potato bugs, apparently immune to Paris green, consumed all the potatoes. After a year of this, the Potato Man took the Paris green himself, and was found as dead as George Washington. Some years ago the house was demolished, and no one means to build upon its site.

At Lost Lake the trail turns east, and you can make your way back toward the village by a different route. An occasional automobile leaves tracks here, going to Blue Lake. So the ruts are well marked; this we call the Sand Road, as distinguished from lesser tracks. Once upon a time the Sand Road was lined with farms, but now only the stumps of poplars, here and there a clump of lilacs, and a few boards remain to mark the sites. A single house still stands, at the junction of the Lost Lake trail and the Sand Road, its steep shingled roof and its concrete walls visible for some distance. By this house is a sycamore; and upon this tree the last tenant of the house was found hanging by the neck, a decade ago. I have told the affair in my short story "Off the Sand Road." This is the most recent violent end in the Lost Lake hinterland. To the dreadful joy of small boys and girls, I refer to the ruin as The House of Death when I am in their company and we pass near.

Farther down the Sand Road, toward the village, a few weather-beaten fragments of siding are the last souvenirs of our most celebrated case two generations gone. Here dwelt the notorious family of Van Tassel. Mr. Van Tassel, like some of our people up the side trails, was a confirmed violator—that is, a poacher; but rumor had it that he did not always confine his shooting to game. Every Sunday he attended the Assembly of God, over toward Remus. One Sunday morning, an eloquent preacher exhorted the congregation to public and immediate confession of sins. Suddenly there rose up Van Tassel, with glowing face; and he cried, "I'll tell it; I'll tell it; I'll tell it if they send me to state's prison!" Every face turned toward him, while minister and congregation waited breathless. But amid this silence, the enthusiasm faded from Van Tassel's unshaven face; he looked coldly and deliberately at the brethren; and then he sat down, unconfessed.

Despite Van Tassel's regularity in attendance at the gospel tabernacle, he always came attired in his dirty old overalls. This the minister endured so long as he could; but after some months, he said to his parishioner, "Mr. Van Tassel, don't you think you should wear better clothes to church on the Lord's Day?"

Van Tassel, regarding him dourly, replied: "Jesus Christ didn't wear no fine clothes."

Thus baffled, the preacher pondered on the question for some days; and presently, meeting Van Tassel in the street, he resumed their discussion. "Mr. Van Tassel, don't you agree that George Washington"—the original, not the Mecosta version—"was a good man?"

"Well, yes."

"Well, George Washington wore fine clothes."

But Van Tassel was not easily vanquished in such doctrinal contests. "Yes," said he, "but hell, that was long 'fore Christ's time."

In the end, Van Tassel died when a large tree fell upon him. He had been cutting down the tree in company with his half-witted son, whom he always had abused; so there was talk. The Van Tassels had several children, one of whom, Lily, went to school with my great-aunts. At school, on one occasion, the children were discussing favorite avocations. "I jes' love to make bread," Lily volunteered. "Your han's allays is so nice an' white after."

Some months later, the Van Tassel children invited classmates home to play with their new doll. This was in the dead of winter. When the guests arrived, they did indeed find the Van Tassel children sliding down hill with a new doll. But that new doll was a human baby, the youngest Van Tassel, dead and frozen stiff. The baby had died the previous week, and had been stored in the woodshed for burial when the frost was out of the ground; the other children had asked if they might have Susan for a doll, and Mrs. Van Tassel had not demurred.

This formidable Mrs. Van Tassel came of the numerous clan of Hunter. The Hunters were what are called Sand Hill Savages. They lived in a collection of shacks away at the back of beyond, up toward Skyberia, and violated and stole after the fashion of the Doones. Their special offense was renting houses. Old Mr. Hunter, head of the clan, could make himself quite presentable by shaving and donning his Sunday blue serge suit. Whenever he heard of a house for rent in a neighboring village—a vacant house with an absentee landlord—he thus adorned himself and sought out the landlord, representing himself as a retired farmer of some means in search of a dwelling in town. If the bargain was concluded, all the Hunters, to an incredible total, moved immediately into the doomed house; they smashed up the partitions for firewood; they broke the panes and fouled the floor; they carried off furniture and curtains. By the time the anguished landlord had obtained their eviction, his property was much depreciated in value.

Now upon the untimely death of her husband, Mrs. Van Tassel took up with an infirm old miser who lived in a shack between Lost Lake and Blue Lake and went to dwell with him, taking the half-witted son with her. This arrangement did not long endure. Some neighbors, passing the cabin of Jones the miser, saw the door standing open and a bloody axe lying on the cabin floor. Search was made for Mr. Jones, who could be found nowhere. Mrs. Van Tassel, who had returned to her previous residence, said that Mr. Jones must have wandered off somewhere. A posse dragged our creeks and lakes, but without success. Then it was whispered that it might be well for the sheriff to drag a second time that deep and snag-choked creek called Dead Stream. When this was done, the body of Jones was found in the mud, his skull crushed. Some suspected that the clan of Hunter had come to the aid of their kinswoman Mrs. Van Tassel, transporting the corpse from hidie-hole to hidie-hole in advance of the posse.

So Mrs. Van Tassel was brought to the bar of justice, and nearly everyone from our township went to hear the testimony. The prosecution claimed that Mrs. Van Tassel had gone to share the bed and board of Mr. Jones with the deliberate design of making an end of him and taking his hoard, while Mrs. Van Tassel pleaded that she had lived with him simply out of pity for his infatuation with her. Mrs. Van Tassel had a peculiarity in her speech: she elided the first syllable of most long words. The prosecutor declared that Mrs. Van Tassel had forced her company on the late Jones; Mrs. Van Tassel retorted that Jones, madly in love with her, had so persisted in his entreaties that at length she had given way: "I 'fused and 'fused, but fin'ly I 'sented."

Our jury roll is made up, in part, of the names of indigent persons, as a means of poor-relief. Between indigence and violating there is a marked coincidence among us. Thus, doubtless libellously, a certain sympathy is said sometimes to subsist between some jurors and the accused. In any event, though the half-witted son (incompetent to testify in a court of law) had spoken of his part in the bashing of Mr. Jones, the jury did not find for the prosecution. When the verdict of "not guilty" was read, Mrs. Van Tassel ran nimbly to the back of the courtroom, cast a glance of withering scorn upon judge, jury, prosecutor, and spectators, thumbed her nose to all, and cried, "Didn't ya get left?" Then she vanished without trace from Mecosta.

No Van Tassels are left now; no one at all dwells along the Sand Road. Even the wild animals have their troubles here. As you trudge back toward the village, you pass on the right a shallow swamp, the scene of an unsuccessful enterprise. The owner of the land conceived a plan for rearing muskrats in this swamp. But in August our fierce droughts nearly dry up this hollow. To solve this difficulty, the entrepreneur dug wells and set over each a windmill, to pump water to the surface and keep his muskrats happy. When August came, nevertheless, the winds did not blow; the windmills did not turn; the water was not pumped; the swamp dried; and the muskrats died or fled. So much for the vanity of human wishes down Lost Lake way.

I own forty acres of woodland and pasture down toward this limbo. There I have endeavored to plant red pines and white pines and white spruces, but the field mice nibble the roots, and the droughts have taken their toll, and the premature spring thaws, with subsequent cold spells, freeze the hopeful sap in my little trees.

A few summers ago, I took to my forty parched acres a friend of mine, a professor of English from Detroit, to make census of the surviving saplings. The weather seemed bent upon vindicating the Pathetic Fallacy; the weather forever does tricks, down Lost Lake way. A mighty wind arose while we walked across one of my desolate fields, making my old grove of sugar maples and elms creak dreadfully; enormous black clouds scudded across the sun; and out of nowhere popped a prodigious groundhog (which creature my friend Peter never had beheld before), running through the trees as if the fiend were coming up through his burrow.

Stopping stock-still, Peter looked cautiously about him, perhaps expecting any moment to catch a glimpse of the Weird Sisters on this blasted heath. "Don't you suppose," he said, precisely but with a certain awe, "we'd best go back to the car?" I understood; and we did.

A Cautionary Note on the Ghostly Tale

To most modern men having ceased to recognize their own souls, the spectral tale is out of fashion, especially in America. As Manning said, all differences of opinion at bottom are theological; and this fact has its bearing upon literary tastes. Because—even though they may be churchgoers—the majority of Americans do not really hunger after personal immortality; they cannot shiver at someone else's fictitious spirit.

Perhaps the cardinal error of the Enlightenment was the notion that dissolving old faiths, creeds, and loyalties would lead to a universal sweet rationalism. But deprive the common man of St. Salvator, and he will seek, at best, St. Science—even though he understands Darwin, say, no better than he understood Augustine. Credulity springs eternal, merely changing its garments from age to age. So if one takes away from man a belief in ghosts, it does not follow that thereafter he will concern himself wholly with Bright Reality; more probably, his fancy will seek some new field— possibly a worse realm.

Thus stories of the supernatural have been supplanted by "science-fiction." Though the talent of H. G. Wells did in that *genre* nearly everything worth undertaking, a flood of "scientific" and "futuristic" fantasies continues to deluge America. With few exceptions, these writings are banal and meaningless. My present point, however, is simply that many people today have a faith in "life in other planets" as burning and genuine as belief in a literal Heaven and a literal Hell was among twelfth-century folk, say—but upon authority far inferior. It is amusing to see physicists like Dr. Harlow Shapley, having abandoned all hope for this world (which obdurately refuses to become Utopia), declare enthusiastically that there *are* people away out yonder, for they have not one shred of scientific evidence. Having demolished, to their own satisfaction, the whole edifice of religious learning, abruptly and unconsciously they experience the need for belief in *something* not mundane; and so, defying their own inductive and mechanistic premises, they take up the cause of Martians and Jovians. As for angels and devils, let alone bogles—why, hell, such notions are superstitious!

But if the stubborn fact remains that although not one well-reputed person claims to have seen the men in the flying saucers, a great many well-reputed persons, over centuries, have claimed to have seen ghosts; or, more strictly speaking, to have perceived certain "psychic phenomena."

From Pliny onward, the literature of our civilization is full of such relations. Scholars have analyzed soberly these appearances, from Father Noel Taillepied's *Treatise on Ghosts* (1588) to Father Herbert Thurston's *Ghosts and Poltergeists* (1955). *The Journal of the Society for Psychical Research* has examined painstakingly, for decades, the data of psychic manifestations. Eminent people so different in character as the Wesleys and Lord Castlereagh have been confronted by terrifying apparitions.

And men of letters have encountered spectral visitants so often as to become altogether casual about these mysteries. Take, as a random example, an aside in Ford Madox Ford's *Portraits from Life*. Ford's London editorial office was in an old house "reputed full of ghosts." Thus—

"My partner Marwood, sitting one evening near the front windows of the room whilst I was looking for something in the drawer of the desk, said suddenly:

" 'There's a woman in lavender-coloured eighteenth-century dress looking over your shoulder into that drawer.' And Marwood was the most matter-of-fact, as it were himself eighteenth-century, Yorkshire Squire that England of those days could have produced."

Ford touches upon this episode merely to introduce his first meeting with D. H. Lawrence, in that office. I suppose that Ford, as indeed he implies, was more embarrassed than alarmed or even interested. For in such matters we always doubt the plain asseverations of our friends and even the testimony of our own senses. Some impression has been made upon the imaginative brain, yes; something extraordinary seems to have happened. But what? Usually the experience is so evanescent and so meaningless, however alarming, that speculations become vain.

That "psychic phenomena" occur even a philosophical materialist like George Santayana took to be indubitable. Santayana's own explanation, or the gist of it, is that in a medium-like state we make out shadows or reflections, as it were, of past events; he writes in *Reason in Religion*,

> "Now the complexity of nature is prodigious; everything that happens leaves, like buried cities, almost indelible traces which an eye, by chance attentive and duly prepared, can manage to read, recovering for a moment the image of an extinct life. Symbols, illegible to reason, can thus sometimes read themselves out in trance and madness. Faint vestiges may be found in matter of forms which it once wore, or which, like a perfume, impregnated and got lodgment within it. Slight echoes may suddenly reconstitute themselves in the mind's silence; and a half-stunned consciousness may catch brief glimpses of long-lost and irrelevant things. Real ghosts are such reverberations of the past, exceeding ordinary imagination and discernment both in vividness and in fidelity . . ."

This is but one analysis of the puzzle, with really no more to substantiate the argument than there is to prove Cicero's suggestions that ghosts are the damned, condemned to linger near the scene of their crimes. Here I am but suggesting, in fine, that no one ever has satisfactorily demonstrated a general theory of ghostly apparitions; yet a mass of testimony of all ages and countries—though particularly abundant, for reasons no one ever has discussed properly, in northern Europe and in Japan and China—exists to inform us that strange things beyond the ordinary laws of life and matter have occurred at irregular intervals and in widely varied circumstances. Two forms of psychic phenomena are fairly frequent: the revenant, and the poltergeist or racketing spirit; and these terrify men. (Telepathy and the milder forms of "second sight" are even more frequently encountered, but they rarely bring with them the horror and dread of the "ghost.")

At the end of his serious book *Apparitions*, Professor G. N. M. Tyrrell remarks, "Psychical research has certainly not drawn a blank. It has, on the contrary, discovered something so big that people sheer away from it in a reaction of fear." This is true; and possibly some day these mystifying events will be properly examined in a scientific spirit, classified, and somehow fitted into the natural sciences—though I doubt it.* At present, such phenomena submit to neither rhyme nor reason: the revenant seems unpredictable and purposeless, and the poltergeist behaves like a feeble-minded child. Thus it is that the True Narration of ghostly happenings almost never attains to the condition of true literature. To guess at any significance in these manifestations, we still have to resort to literary art—that is, to fiction. And art, after all, is man's nature.

Because this limbo has no defined boundaries and interiorly remains *terra incognita*, the imaginative writer's fancy can wander there unburdened by the dreary impedimenta of twentieth-century naturalism. For symbol and allegory, the shadow-world is a far better realm than the

* Suppose, suggests C. E. M. Joad, that we appoint a sober committee of three to sit in the haunted room at midnight and take notes on the appearance of the ghost. But suppose also that one of the conditions necessary for ghostly phenomena is that there *not* be present a sober committee of three: well, then, the very scientific method has precluded the possibility of obtaining scientific results.

hard, false "realism" of science fiction. A return to the ghostly and the Gothick might be one rewarding means of escape from the exhausted lassitude and inhumanity of the typical novel or short story of the Sixties. Unlike the True Narration, the fictional ghostly tale can possess plot, theme, and purpose. It can piece together in some pattern the hints which seem thrown out by this or that vision or haunting or case of second-sight. It can touch keenly upon the old reality of evil—and upon injustice and retribution. It can reveal aspects of human conduct and longing to which the positivistic psychologist has blinded himself. And it still can be a first-rate yarn.

* * *

What makes a ghostly tale worth reading—or writing? Certainly the supernatural has attracted writers of genius or high talent: Defoe, Scott, Coleridge, Stevenson, Kipling, the Sitwells; Hawthorne, Poe, Henry James, F. Marion Crawford, Edith Wharton; and those whose achievement lies principally in this field, among them M. R. James, Algernon Blackwood, Meade Faulkner, Sheridan Le Fanu, and Arthur Machen. Some of the best stories are by such poets and critics as de la Mare, A. C. Benson, and Quiller-Couch. These are no Grub-Street names. The *genre* contains something worthy of art.

A fearful joy clearly is one attraction, from Horace Walpole to L. P. Hartley. Most of us enjoy being scared, so long as we are reasonably confident that nothing dreadful really will overtake us. Thus the fun of the Gothick tale is the fun of the roller coaster or the crazy-house at the county fair. It is worth remarking that the grand milieu of the ghost story was in nineteenth-century Europe, and especially

England. Despite its revolutionary changes, the last century now seems to us an age of security and normality; and England particularly was safe and cozy. The Christmas ghost story, told by the blazing fire, with all the strong defenses of a rich and triumphant civilization to reassure the timorous, reached its apogee in the delightful frights of Montague Rhodes James, provost of Eton, shortly before the First World War.

Yet this is not the whole of the matter; if it were, supernatural fictions would have short shrift in our age. The fountains of the great deep being broken up in our time, we have supped long on real horrors, and require no fanciful alarums to titillate our palates. Gauleiter and commissar are worse than spectral raw-head-and-bloody-bones. What is nearly as bad, man in modern fiction—as Mr. Edmund Fuller has pointed out—tends toward a depravity more shocking than Monk Lewis' grotesqueries. The august schools of Mr. Dashiell Hammett and Mr. James M. Cain provide for appetites that find phantasms not sufficiently carnal. And for those who are after pure, and relatively harmless, diversion, the daily slaughter in the Wild West of television may suffice. Without straining credulity, no ghost could do half so much mischief as a Private Eye.

Notwithstanding these handicaps, the tale of the supernatural, I fancy, will endure as a minor form of genuine literary art, perhaps occasionally emerging—as in *The Turn of the Screw*—as a vehicle for powerful insights. For at its best the uncanny romance touches upon certain profound truths: upon the dark powers that aspire always to possess us, and upon intimations of immortality.

Mr. Gerald Heard once said to me that the good ghost

story must have for its base some clear premise as to the character of human existence—some theological assumption. A notable example of such a story is Heard's own best piece of fiction, which I believe to be the most impressive supernatural tale of recent years: "The Chapel of Ease," a long short story of a mystical Anglo-Catholic parson who prays for the tormented souls of gallows crows, their bones laid beneath his ancient and half-derelict chapel. Rising in the pews, their ghosts hate the man who struggles to save them; and in the end the pain of the contest is too much for the priest, and he dies. All this is told with a chilly power peculiar to a writer himself a mystic and a poet.

George Macdonald and his disciple C. S. Lewis employ the ghostly and supernatural means in letters for a moral and theological end; and from them the rising generation of authors ought to learn that naturalism is not the only road to higher reality. Indeed, for the writer who struggles to express moral truth, "realism" has become in our time a dead-end street; it fully deserves now the definition in Ambrose Bierce's *Devil's Dictionary:* "The art of depicting nature as it is seen by toads. The charm suffusing a landscape painted by a mole, or a story written by a measuring-worm."

Amid nineteenth-century meliorism, Emerson never could credit the reality of evil. But a good many twentieth-century writers are unable to credit the reality of anything except evil. Now it can be said of the better ghostly tale that it is underlain by a sound concept of the character of evil. Defying nature, the necromancer conjures up what ought not to rise again this side of Judgment Day. But these dark powers do not rule the universe; they are in rebellion against natural order; and by bell, book, and candle, literally or symbolically, we can push them down under. This truth runs through the priest's ghost stories in A. C. Benson's *The Light Invisible;* also it is implied in some of the eerie narrations of W. B. Yeats' *Mythologies.*

I venture to suggest that the more orthodox is a writer's theology, the more convincing, as symbols and allegories, his uncanny tales will be. One of the most unnerving of all spooky stories is Algernon Blackwood's "The Damned," which takes place in an ugly modern house where the cellars seem to be full of souls in torment, doled out little drops of water by the medium-housekeeper. But in its concluding pages—and this is true of too many of Blackwood's creations—the power of the story is much diminished when the reader is informed that, after all, the cellars aren't really Hell: it is merely that people who formerly lived in the house *believed* in Hell and so invested the place with an unpleasant aura. Because the Christian tradition, with its complex of symbol, allegory, and right reason, genuinely penetrates to spiritual depths and spiritual heights, the modern supernatural story which isolates itself from this authority drifts aimlessly down Styx.

Though Freudianism retains great popular influence today, as an intellectual force it is nearly spent; and Freud's naïve understanding of human nature must make way for older and greater insights. For Freudians and positivists, only the "natural" exists. The philosophical and ideological currents of a period necessarily affecting its imaginative literature, the supernatural in fiction has been somewhat ridiculous much of this century. But as the rising generation regains the awareness that "nature" is something more than mere fleshly sensation, and that something lies both above and below human nature—that reality, when all's said, is hierarchical—then authors may venture once more to employ myth and symbol, to resort to allegories of the divine and the diabolical as lawful literary instruments. And in this revival the ghostly tale may have its part. *Tenebrae* ineluctably form part of the nature of things.

But enough; I am turning into a ghostly comforter. I do not ask the artist in the fantastic to turn didactic moralist; and I trust that he will not fall into the error that the shapes under the hill are symbols *merely*. For the sake of his art, the author of ghostly narrations ought never to enjoy freedom from fear. As that formidable moralist Samuel Johnson lived in dread of real eternal torment—not mere "mental anguish"—so the "invisible prince," Sheridan Le Fanu, archetype of ghost-story writers, is believed to have died literally of fright. He knew that his creations were not his creations merely, but glimpses of the abyss.

And I hope that in writing Gothick romances for moderns who suffer from *taedium vitae*, the coming set of eerie authors will not modernize their craft beyond recognition. It has been a skill innately conservative. As M. R. James wrote of Le Fanu, "The ghost story is in itself a slightly old-fashioned form; it needs some deliberateness in the telling; we listen to it the more readily if the narrator poses as elderly, or throws back his experience to 'some thirty years ago.' " If faithless to this trust, the ghost-story creator will deserve to be hounded to his doom by the late James Thurber's favorite monster, the Todal, "a creature of the Devil, sent to punish evildoers for having done less evil than they should."

No longer the property of the
Boston Public Library.
Sale of this material benefits the Library

Boston Public Library
Central Library, Copley Square

Copley Square
General Library

The Date indicates the book should be returned. Please do not remove from this pocket.

PZ
.K595SU

11543096

Contents of
THE SURLY SULLEN BELL
include . . .

"Uncle Isaiah": A racketeer gets an unexpected pay-off. . . .

"Off the Sand Road": It is not advisable to violate a sign reading "No Trasepsing."

"Ex Tenebris": A planning officer meets an unusual kind of resistance—the mortal kind!

"The Surly Sullen Bell": Old loves linger in the lurking presence of a subtle danger. . . .

"Skyberia": Two hunters lose their way in the wilderness and discover the threat of their own civilization.

"Sorworth Place": A traveler in Scotland falls in love with a ghost's widow and is appropriately rewarded.

"Behind the Stumps": A persistent census-taker strays too far afield and crosses the border between the living and the dead.

"What Shadows We Pursue": The spirit of a bibliophile speaks through 12,000 books and takes its revenge in an unusual manner.

"Lost Lake": A true account of a cold, black, legend-inspiring lake without an outlet.

"The Cellar of Little Egypt": Violence and local color participate equally.

A Cautionary Note on the Ghostly Tale, the concluding essay, is a brilliant and sparkling analysis of the genre in the light of varying traditions.

By the same author:

OLD HOUSE OF FEAR $3.95

FLEET PUBLISHING CORPORATION
230 Park Avenue, New York

CPSIA information can be obtained
at www.ICGtesting.com
Printed in the USA
BVHW030736130822
644447BV00010BA/173